The Mushroom Picker

Lyle N. Solland

PublishAmerica
Baltimore

© 2005 by Lyle N. Solland.
All rights reserved. No part of this book may be reproduced, stored in a retrieval system or transmitted in any form or by any means without the prior written permission of the publishers, except by a reviewer who may quote brief passages in a review to be printed in a newspaper, magazine or journal.

First printing

At the specific preference of the author, PublishAmerica allowed this work to remain exactly as the author intended, verbatim, without editorial input.

ISBN: 1-4137-8076-8
PUBLISHED BY PUBLISHAMERICA, LLLP
www.publishamerica.com
Baltimore

Printed in the United States of America

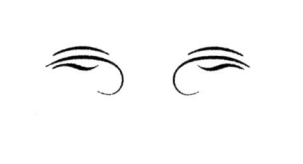

The screen door banged shut and Kat raced into the living room like a fury. Gramps and Gram were startled by the interruption to their otherwise peaceful evening.

"I got a car," Kat said, as if she were the first person on the planet to actually own one.

After a brief pause, Gram said, "Where did you get a car, dear?"

"From a friend of mine who bought a new one. They wouldn't give him a trade-in, so he sold it to me."

"How are you going to pay for it?" asked Gramps as politely as an old rancher could.

"I've got a job at Smiley's Burgers now, so I'll give him fifty dollars a month until it's paid for," Kat said proudly.

"We'd better go check it out," Gramps muttered, thinking to himself that women should not really be allowed to buy cars. They just did not know what to look for. He was nonetheless very proud of his granddaughter.

They walked out of the kitchen and looked questioningly at the tiny green car parked in front.

Kat ran over and yelled, "You drive, Gramps!" as she hopped into the back seat.

Gramps and Gram got in and slammed the doors as if they were in their old pickup truck.

"It's a four speed," said Kat, as Gramps grabbed the wheel and squeezed himself in. He fired the tiny engine up and away they went. Gramps shifted up through the gears like an old pro. Gravel pinged off the bottom, giving the effect of riding in a tin can, but the little car dipped and dived around the potholes like it had been trained. At the corner Gramps and Gram switched sides and Gram proudly drove the new car back to the ranch.

"I'll make some tea," Gram said, as Gramps and Kat began their mechanical inspection.

They tinkered and cleaned for an hour before Gramps finally said, "She looks pretty good from the outside, Kat, and you look like you're getting too skinny and need some of Gram's cookin'."

Gram had the table set and all three of them had their own favorite chair. Gram had set out a feast, as she always did when company was there. They had sandwiches and homemade pie with ice cream before they slid their chairs back.

Gram spoke first. "Heard from your Dad?"

Kat's father and mother had divorced the year before and her father, Stan, had married a woman with three children of her own.

Stan was the second of two sons born to Gramps and Gram. His older brother had died when Stan was fourteen, and Stan had never stopped missing him.

There was no room in his life now for Kat and the new wife made sure that this was clearly understood. She now controlled his every move.

Kat showed a twinge of sadness. "Yeah, yesterday. He's still being bossed around by that cow he calls his wife. He wants to come out here for a couple of days but she won't allow it. Boy, if I ever get married I sure hope I don't find somebody like that."

"The Cow," as Kat called her, had expensive tastes. She spent and borrowed faster than Stan could bring the money in. Every once in a while he would have to call Gramps to bail him out of a credit card bill.

Gram smiled lovingly at Kat and said, "We all make mistakes sometimes, dear. I'm sure your father loves you very much and would spend every day with you if he could."

"Yeah, I know, Gram," Kat said, not wanting to upset her.

"You got plates on your car yet?" asked Gramps.

"No, gotta wait 'til I get some money for plates and insurance before I drive her," Kat said sadly. They all sat quietly, deep in thought.

"Your Granddad is getting too old to handle all of these cattle by himself, Kat. Maybe we can hire you once in a while. You're a better cowboy than anybody else I can think of."

Kat grinned and said, "When do I start?" and laughed as she mumbled,

"Do I need to bring a lunch?"

Gram glared and then chuckled. Nobody had ever brought a lunch to the Townsend house.

"Needs tires. I'll go to town in the morning and get some, and if you come in after school we'll get the plates. Then you'll be fixed up and ready to roll. If you want to stay the night I'll drive you to school in the morning," Gramps said.

"Yeah, I'd rather be anywhere than at Mom's. Her boyfriend is a jerk." So it was settled.

After supper, Gramps and Kat sat on the top rail in the late spring evening, looking over the ranch. The big herd bull and a big pig were lying on the hillside, sunning themselves.

"I see old Sprig is still doing fine," Kat said looking at the pig.

Sprig was a sow that had escaped from a neighbor's place when he was loading his truck to get out of the hog business. She had wandered over to Gramps' ranch and became buddies with the big bull. They went everywhere together. In the winter she slept in the bull shed, or, if it turned really cold, she would tunnel into the bales and hole up until it warmed up.

Shortly after she had arrived, Gram had decided that she needed a name, and Kat had come up with "Sprig".

"Where on earth did you ever come up with that name?" Gram had asked.

"It is short for Spoiled Rotten Pig," Kat had laughed, and the name had stuck. Sprig became Gram's pet, and wandered to the old farmhouse every afternoon for the kitchen scraps that Gram gave her.

Gramps looked out at his herd and said, "You really have to watch that black one when she calves. Actually, Kat, watch them all.

"If you go out with them when they calf, always carry a big stick and be prepared to use it. If you ever let them get the best of you they'll end up hurting you some day."

This was Gramps' cattle watching lecture that she got whenever he surveyed the herd.

"Never trust a bull. Sprig, maybe."

Kat had her own special room in Gram's old farmhouse. She had treasures on the shelves and her pictures covered the walls. Her sister was quiet and more reserved, so she did not like the farm, where work always came first. She would rather read a book. They had an older brother who was gay, which did not sit well with Gramps.

Kat was their special one and always would be. She followed Gramps wherever he went, and had slowly learned everything about operating a ranch. She had midwifed the cows, driven the tractors, branded the calves and castrated the bulls, and was becoming quite the carpenter. Gramps was proud.

After sleeping like a log and devouring a huge breakfast, Kat hopped in the old truck with Gramps, and they began their journey to town. Every trip with Gramps was a lesson in local history, wildlife, agriculture, road construction or world politics. His pickup was an old Chevy with the spare tire mounted in the front. Everybody for miles around knew that truck.

"Why don't you get a new truck?" asked Kat as they chugged along.

"Don't need one. I'm just getting this old girl figured out," laughed Gramps.

They laughed at themselves and teased each other the rest of the way, waving to everyone they met.

Kat had a final exam and did not want to be late. The test was two hours long but she found it easy.

The final bell rang and Kat raced out to meet Gramps. They headed over to the Government Building and hurried to the vehicle office.

The lady at the counter asked what they needed and Kat said proudly, "I'd like to register my new car," as though she had just purchased a new Jaguar.

"May I have your name and age, please," the lady said, as she filled out the form.

"Kathy Rae Townsend, 18," Kat said in a hurry to get the paperwork finished.

"Address?"

"Box 27, Cremona, Alberta, Canada." She gave Gramps' address.

They stopped the truck on the way home to watch a young bull moose grazing in the willows and Gramps whispered, "I'll have to give that miserable old goat, Judge Thacker, a call and tell him about this one. He'd look good in a freezer."

The Judge and Gramps had been pals for years, but unless you knew them, you would think they despised each other from the hard time they gave one another.

They stopped again to check the hay on the creek quarter and dropped salt off for the steers at the Home Place.

"Got a couple bulls that I bought last fall that need fixin'. Wonderin' if you could come over Saturday and we'll castrate them and knock the horns off a couple of heifers?"

"Sure," said Kat, even though she wanted to go to the mall with her friends.

Kat ran to her car, admiring the new tires Gramps had put on, and noticed that the tank was now full. She waved good-bye as she sped down the driveway.

Kat loaded up as many friends as her little car would hold, picked up cokes and ice cream, and they paraded up and down Main Street for two hours.

Towards evening, Kat finally had to go home. She lived at her mother's place just out of town. The place was not old, but already run down. It belonged to the people that owned the bar in town, and because her mother spent most of her money there, they gave her a break on the rent.

Kat's mother drank and gambled, and many nights Kat had gone hungry because there was not enough money left for food. Last month she had brought some loser boyfriend home and he had been hanging around ever since. Kat did not like him at all. She only knew his name as Dean something.

Kat sneaked quietly in and began her homework. She was an honor student in spite of her parents. She had not been home long when the door slammed and the yelling began. They were both drunk and fighting about something. Kat hoped that they did not know that she was home.

"Kat!" her mother yelled.

"What?" was Kat's response.

"Whose car is that?"

"Oh, it's just a friend's car," Kat lied, so they would not ask to borrow it.

"Why is it here?" she asked.

"Wouldn't start," was Kat's reply.

"Tell them to get the God-damned thing out of here or I'll call the cops," yelled Dean something.

"OK," said Kat, maintaining her composure as she thought, "Never, you drunken fool."

Kat went back to her homework and they forgot about her as they bickered on and on.

The next morning, when Kat arrived at the ranch, Gram knew by instinct that something was wrong.

"Hi Kat," she said. "How are things with you today?"

"Oh, all right," Kat replied, quietly.

Gramps and Gram looked at each other knowing that Kat had no real home and she was not even welcome anywhere but at the ranch.

"What a shame," they thought, "when the parents are so selfish that they neglect a kid like Kat."

The cowboys started arriving early on Friday afternoon. Branding day on the ranch was a major event that Gramps' and Gram's friends looked forward to each year. Within a few hours, the yard was filled with everything from shiny new motor homes to old yellow school buses. Horses were tied to anything that would hold them. The women packed pots and trays of food to feed the small army.

Kat laughed as she watched a bunch of kids playing with Sprig. She was having as much fun as they were, running around the barnyard just fast enough to keep from getting caught. Many of the old cowboys had brought their grandchildren with them for the weekend. The old men were scattered around the yard in small groups, each one sporting a battered cowboy hat that was unique to him.

One group was giving a new horse their closest attention, lifting one foot after another, then checking his teeth. Another was looking at the blue mountains on the horizon while one man described an elk-hunting trip on which he had bagged a trophy animal. A very old man was looking at an ancient tractor with trees growing up through the openings, while describing to his grandsons the years when he had driven one like that. The women busied themselves on the patio and chattered to everyone in general and no one in particular.

Just before dark, the Indians arrived from the local reserve. Gramps always told Kat that they were some of the best cowboys that he had ever seen. The older folks had campers and trailers but the grandchildren all set up their tents. The kids all tried to get Sprig to come over and sleep in their tent, but she was having too much fun.

Kat heard the chainsaws fire up and watched as one dead tree after another fell to the ground. Soon a few old cowboys came riding in, each dragging a tree with his lariat dallied around his saddle horn. Kids ran over and removed their loops from the trees so they could return for another load. More chainsaws fired up and some men began bucking the trees into lengths while others chopped and piled. Before long, there was a huge pile of firewood next to a roaring campfire.

Food covered the tables, and everyone dug in until they were stuffed. Then the paper plates were thrown into the fire. Sparks climbed high into the dark sky above.

A fellow stepped into the firelight with his guitar and began to strum quietly. Within a few minutes there were several old cowboys playing guitars while one of the old Indians played the fiddle. Somebody asked him to play some Bach and the old fellow broke into a classical violin solo. Kat stood wide-eyed and almost unable to believe what she was watching. The most wonderful music was coming from the violin. The woman beside her told Kat that he had learned from the radio. The old man smiled when he was finished and began to play country tunes again.

A bunch of kids ran by the campfire and the grandmothers unleashed a torrent of scolding. The children were long gone and did not hear a word they said. The tunes played on and on. Kat watched a flashlight moving around in a large tent where the kids had all congregated to tell ghost stories. She laughed as she heard the screams when the children scared themselves with their terrifying stories. She was sure the tent would collapse within the hour.

Kat watched Sprig walk by the flickering campfire, stood up, and led her to the barn for the night. Sprig followed Kat into the barn and politely took the sandwich Kat offered her. When Kat walked out, she noticed an old man leaning against a fence rail.

"Hi, MoJo," she said, walking to him.

"Hi, Kathy," he said. "Sure is a beautiful night. Just been here lookin' at the stars. They're sure bright tonight. My hearin' aid bothers me around all that racket so I came out here for a while."

"Yeah," Kat replied. "Look at the Big Dipper. You can almost touch it tonight."

"Folks been followin' that old North Star for thousands of years," MoJo said. "Without it our ancestors would have been lost."

"Where is it?" Kat asked.

"It's easy to find," said MoJo. "You just take five times the length of the dipper on the Big Dipper and follow it up. See? It's right there."

"Well isn't that something!" Kat said. "I never knew that, MoJo."

"Those stars in a line up there with those going down at an angle, that's Orion's Belt. The constellation is called Orion. In the Northern Hemisphere we can navigate by the North Star but they can't see it South of the equator. The ancient Polynesians steered their boats by Orion, but it moves in the sky so it's a lot harder to navigate by."

"Where did you learn all that stuff, MoJo?" Kat asked.

"I worked on ships when I was your age, Kathy," he said. "I traveled all around the world before I finally settled here."

"Why here?" Kat asked.

"I met a young lady and brought her to the most wonderful place in the world. You should travel the world while you're still young. When you come back here you'll understand. I still miss the ocean sometimes but I wouldn't trade."

Kat and MoJo stood for a long time watching the stars sparkle high above the distant mountains while the music echoed from the cowboys that surrounded the campfire. Grandmothers bustled around the tent village trying to sort the children into their respective tents. They finally gave up and returned to the fire. The festivities eventually wound up and the fires were doused as people returned to their campers to get as much rest as possible for the busy day ahead.

Kat was up at the crack of dawn, but the old timers were already preparing for the day. Frying pans were sizzling on barbecues with stacks of bacon while others held eggs and pancakes. Gram was busy filling paper plates and passing them out to anybody that was hungry. A pail full of coffee hung on a tripod over the campfire. Kat hurried out to help Gram serve their unpaid helpers. When breakfast was almost over Kat saddled her roan and Gramps' big black gelding. They stood quietly at the hitching rail with the many horses that the old cowboys had brought with them. One of Gramps' old friends came over leading a quiet old sorrel, while a teenaged girl followed, leading a hot-blooded Arab. Kat thought that she must be Miss Rodeo or something with all the fancy western clothes.

Kat overheard the old fellow say, "You'd better take those spurs off, young lady. They'll get you in trouble."

"I'm fine, Grandpa," she replied. "I just wear them for show." Kat had noticed the beautiful set of Mexican silver spurs with large pointed rowels.

The cowboys left the yard in a loose bunch heading down toward the creek with Gramps in the lead. Some of them were getting pretty old but Kat marvelled at the way they handled their horses. She could tell that they were doing what they enjoyed.

The Miss Rodeo girl was a fairly good rider but her horse was a bit too spirited for her. It kept prancing and throwing its head, making her life difficult. When she was about to cross a little dip in the cow trail, her horse hunched up and lunged across. The girl lifted a few inches in the saddle and her spurs came up into the Arab's belly. The horse exploded, bucking and kicking across the pasture before she could get a grip on the saddle horn. She was bucked out of the saddle on the first jump, and came down on the horse's rump. When he bucked again the girl was catapulted high into the air.

She flew through the air, landing in a pile of cow manure beside the trail.

She pulled herself up, horrified when she saw that she was covered in it.

Her Grandpa watched long enough to be sure she wasn't hurt, then tore off after the Arab at a full gallop, shaking out a loop in his lariat as he went. When he got close enough, he twirled the loop and settled it around the Arab's neck. He dallied the rope around his saddle horn and brought the big sorrel around. When the Arab hit the end of the rope it twanged but held. The old cowboy led him over to a tree and tied him to it.

"You can spend the whole day right here, you knothead!" he said. "No good for nothing...," he muttered.

He rode back to where his granddaughter stood stinking to high Heaven, her new clothes ruined. She tearfully climbed up behind him to go back to the house and clean up.

The cowboys rode slowly down by the creek and began chasing the cows from the trees to where they were bunched in an open meadow. When they had them all, they pressed them gradually to the barnyard and into the corral.

Kat tied her horse before getting the branding irons ready. She had the hard job today. The cowboys would rope the calves and lead them up to where they were waiting. Then Kat and a young fellow would flip the calves and stretch them out. One cowboy branded, another vaccinated them, another cowboy removed their horns and then the veterinarian surgically castrated the bulls. Kat did not look the part of a cowboy with her worn out sneakers and baseball cap on backwards, red hair poking out from underneath, and was filthy by the time the day had barely begun. She was kicked and bunted but she worked like a trooper.

They did not stop until the last calf was branded. Gram came down once in a while with a clean pail to put the testicles in, so she could prepare them for the barbecue tonight. The old cowboys worked like a well-oiled machine, with everyone doing their assigned task. Kat knew they were a dying breed. This surely was not the modern way.

Every muscle hurt by the time Kat finally finished. She cleaned up the branding irons and equipment, while the cowboys unsaddled their horses. Somebody handed Kat a beer when she walked by and she downed it in seconds. She went into the house to wash, and found Gram and her pals in the kitchen getting supper ready for the gang.

Kat laughed when she looked in the mirror. She was covered in dust and cow manure, and she appeared to be anything but a lady. Kat scrubbed until she was as clean as a whistle before she headed outside to join the rest.

The women had the barbecue burning and were beginning to cook the prairie oysters. They looked better all cleaned and lightly breaded. There were steaks as well for the guests.

"This is beef country," Gram said with a laugh.

The kids lined up to get the prairie oysters hot off the grill. As soon as they were finished the first helping, they were back for seconds. Gram finally had to make them eat something else so there would be some left for the older folks.

Kat filled a heaping plate with delicious food and settled into a lawn chair. She was sure that even more muscles had started aching. She polished off the food and sat back to enjoy the evening.

Gramps' two older bachelor neighbors came over to sit beside Kat. They were brothers who had never married, and had just stayed on the farm. Kat liked them because they were both such gentlemen.

"You did well today, Kathy," one said. "If I wasn't getting so darned old, I'd have spelled you off, but they'd have to carry me home."

"We had to get rid of our cows," said the other one. "You should take over the ranch, Kathy. You're getting to be pretty handy around here. We could help you get goin'."

"I'll have to think about that," Kat replied. "Thanks for the offer, but as sore as I'm getting right now, the last thing I want is to see another calf."

The guitars and fiddles came out for the evening's entertainment, much to Kat's delight. Children ran back and forth around the yard as the sun slowly sank over the mountains. Sparks from the campfire rose into the night sky, floating higher and higher until they burned themselves out. Folks sang along whenever they knew the words to a song. Kat's eyes fluttered until she fell sound asleep, tired and happy.

Kat awoke with a start. The woman beside her yelled, "That silly old fool. I thought he went to the trailer to rest hours ago. He must have walked all the way down to the pasture to get that stupid horse. The old bugger's over seventy and has no business doing things like that. He thinks he's still a kid."

Kat looked over and watched the old cowboy riding up on his granddaughter's Arab. The horse was jumpy and getting worse as it approached the campfire where people were singing and clapping. She noticed a slight smile appear on the old man's face when he got close, and watched as he let the reins go slack. The Arab instantly dropped its head and let fly with both hind feet.

"Why, that old fool. He's just showing off. One of these days he's going to wind up in the hospital. Watch him, he'll buck that stupid, good for nothing horse right through the campfire. I've seen it before and he always claims that he's just hanging on for dear life, but I know better." The horse bucked high in the air, trying to unseat the old cowboy, but he just sat there and made it look easy.

"Just like he was ridin' a rockin' chair," one old fellow said. The horse bucked closer until he was finally kicking the logs in the campfire. People scrambled away as the sparks flew high into the night sky. The old fellow finally hauled back on the reins, and several of the cowboys grabbed the bridle and held it while he got off, removing the battered cowboy hat and bowing as the onlookers clapped and cheered.

He walked over to sit beside his wife.

"You stupid ass," she scolded. "You could have been hurt, you're too old for that. You should know better and I'm selling that knothead the minute I get home."

"Yes, dear," he replied, winking and grinning at Kat, carefully, so the old lady did not see.

"Where did you learn to ride like that?" Kat asked.

"I used to ride in the rodeos when I was younger. That's how I put myself through University. I just can't seem to get it out of my blood, even though I run a corporation now and have to wear a suit.

"It may sound funny but the decisions you make on a bronc are as hard as business decisions, but you haven't got much time and you land a lot harder if you make the wrong one. My wife's right though. I guess one of these days I'm going to have to hang up my saddle, but I'm sure going to hate to."

"Maybe just stay off the broncs," Kat laughed. "Stick to your saddle horse and you'll be fine."

"Don't give the old coot any ideas," his wife said. "Next thing you know he'll be buying a ranch of his own."

The guitars and fiddles resumed their lively tunes, much to the delight of the onlookers. Kat slipped quietly away and went to bed.

The next morning they sat quietly on the top corral rail for a long time. Gramps quietly interrupted Kat's trance.

"I want you to have this." He handed his old jackknife to Kat. "My dad gave it to me when I was about your age and it has served me well. Keep the middle blade the sharpest for working the bulls."

"Thanks," Kat replied. She did not like serious conversations but could feel one building.

"Sure hope the ranch will be yours one day. You're the only one that knows how to run it. If your dad had better taste for women that would help." Gramps did not hold back when he got started on something.

"Your mother was drunk all the time so the place would have gone to buy booze and that stupid thing he's with now, she's just like that useless cow over there. Bossy, too fat, can't even raise a decent calf. By the way, she goes to town this fall. Any ideas, Kat?"

"Yeah, I'm starving," she replied, laughing as she watched Gram step onto the veranda.

Gram had a meal fit for royalty laid out on the table. They chattered as they ate, and commented on there being no Spam on the table. Gram always bragged that whatever they ate was grown right there on the ranch.

"You must be about done with school," said Gram.

"Yeah," Kat replied, trying hard not to let her sadness show. She had opted out of all of her graduation ceremonies because of her parents. She could just picture her mother showing up drunk with Dean in tow. Her dad would be welcome, but he would have insisted on bringing that fat, loud-mouthed wife of his, and maybe a couple of her ugly offspring. This would have been too much to handle and besides, she was not one for formalities anyway.

She did not even have a escort. If they did not measure up to Gramps, she dumped them. She was not going to spend the rest of her life with somebody who could not hold his own. It all made sense for Kat to miss her graduation, but nonetheless it saddened her.

"You goin' to college?" Gramps asked.

"No, I think I'm going to work for a while and try to save up some money," Kat said.

"Girls need an education nowadays, unless you want to work for minimum wage. It's not fair, but it's reality," muttered Gramps.

"When you decide that you're goin', we'll give you a bit of money to help with expenses," Gram piped up.

"Why wait 'til then?" said Gramps. "We'll open a bank account for you one of these days, and when I sell the calves this fall I'll add a bit. That way you'll be a bit ahead when you start."

"What are you thinking of taking?" asked Gram.

"I'm thinking of taking psychology," said Kat. "I'd really like to know why people do what they do and say what they say."

"Would anybody pay you to do that?" asked Gramps.

"Yeah," said Kat. "Big companies hire psychologists now so they have more insight into the people they hire. May save them from hiring somebody who has a good resume, and is good at job interviews, but is not very good at his job. Some people have a bad temper or can't interact with other workers. A good psychologist can see through all that."

The conversation was getting too serious for Kat so she added, "Maybe I can give my dad a lesson on women. He needs it." They all laughed and tried to imitate her selfish stepmother.

"Hope nobody is watching us," giggled Gram. "They'll think we've lost our minds." As the night wore on they ventured off to their rooms with happy thoughts.

On Sunday, Kat drove her little car to Calgary to visit her dad. She had not driven very much, and the city of a million people scared her. She hated cities anyway but it was the only way that she could see her dad. She left early in the morning to beat the rush.

When she got there, she rang the doorbell and waited. She rang it again, and waited for what seemed an eternity. There was a brand new Buick parked in the driveway beside her dad's old truck, and she wondered how much her dad had borrowed to buy it.

Finally she banged on the door. Kat was not a very patient person. A scruffy looking kid opened the door and just stood there.

"My dad here?" asked Kat.

The boy turned his back and walked back into the house. He said nothing, and Kat thought that he looked a bit slow. She looked in the kitchen and noticed that the sink was piled high with dirty dishes, and the counters were covered with pizza boxes and half-eaten TV dinners.

"Gramps' barn is cleaner than this place," Kat thought, as she surveyed the mess.

Dad came out of a room in the back and Kat ran over and gave him a big hug.

He looked at her and said. "Kat, you've grown up since I saw you last. You look great."

He quickly began a stream of questions: "Seen Mom and Dad? Is your Mom still drinking? Are Mom and Dad ever going to retire? How's school?"

He would have kept going but Kat interrupted, "We're all good, Dad. How about you?"

"OK," he answered, uneasily. "Would you like some coffee?"

He pushed aside the Styrofoam plates and cardboard boxes until he got to the coffee maker. He rinsed it, started the coffee and sat back down beside Kat.

"I've been trying to get out to the ranch for a couple of days to help Dad, but just haven't had the time," he said.

"Yeah," Kat replied, thinking about his controlling wife.

"You must be about finished school? What about your graduation?" her dad asked.

"Yeah, I finish in a couple weeks and decided that I wasn't going to any ceremonies. I'm not much for formal stuff, you know," Kat answered, trying not to show any emotion whatsoever. As she finished, a door opened, and out stomped her dad's new wife.

"What a pathetic sight," Kat thought.

"Can't you two keep the noise down a bit?" she roared. "Don't you know I was up late watching a movie? Stan, you have to take Jacob to his video club meeting in ten minutes so you'd better get moving."

Dad said quietly, "But, Sheila, Kat's here to visit me today. Couldn't you take him?"

"Can't you hear?" Sheila snapped. "I told you I was tired and you can do something for your son once in a while."

She glared at Kat.

"I have to go soon anyway," Kat lied. "Just stopped in for a minute to say hi."

"You can stay and visit with Sheila for a bit," her dad said, as he walked out the door.

As soon as the door had closed, Sheila moved in front of Kat and growled, "This is my house now and this is my family. You are not part of my family and are not welcome here. I never want to see you here again. Your father is finished with his previous marriage and any commitments that go with it and has me now. He doesn't want or need you any more so don't call. When we meet in public we ignore each other. Understood?"

Kat was thunderstruck. She knew that Sheila was selfish, but never quite realized to what extent. "What would Gramps do now?" she asked herself, as she gathered her thoughts.

"You fat bitch!" she burst out. "I'll call my dad whenever and wherever I feel like and if you get in my way you'll lose, I'll guarantee that. And you can kiss my ass!" she yelled, as she slammed the door in Sheila's face and stomped to her car. She drove a couple of blocks before she pulled over and vibrated in anger.

Kat walked out of the school with mixed emotions. She liked being a kid. Responsibility and planning were definitely not her greatest attributes. She always liked to wing it. That's when she was happiest, just enjoying the moment.

"You going down to the river?" asked Sal. "A bunch of us are having a wind up party tonight, so you'd better come. Just bring whatever you want to drink."

"Thanks," Kat replied. "All right if I just drink coke? I just can't drink alcohol, makes me sick."

"Sure, but I love the stuff. Makes me sick too, but only if I make a pig of myself," Sal said with a laugh.

Kat walked slowly to her little Firefly and eased it out of the parking lot. Some boys drove past her in a pickup, yelling and waving their beer, already feeling the effects.

Kat drove down the dusty gravel roads that led toward the ranch, contemplating her future plans. She finally laughed at herself and tossed her schoolbooks into the back seat. Tonight she was finished school, and she was going to enjoy herself.

Gramps and Gram were sitting at the table when she walked in. Gram sprang out of her chair to get Kat fresh buns and coffee.

"Well, I'm finished school now and I'll have to find a job," Kat said. "I guess I'd better start looking around."

"There's no hurry," said Gramps. "Enjoy your youth while you have it. You'll have a lot of years to be old."

"Yes, dear," Gram added, "have some fun while you're young."

"I'm going to a party down by the river tonight," Kat said. "That should be lots of fun."

The spring days were long, but the sun was dipping over the mountains when Kat drove into the meadow beside the river. She pulled her lawn chair and cooler from the little car and sat down beside the roaring campfire.

Music boomed from huge speakers that sat in the back of a pickup. Young people came and went. They were young and ready to face whatever the world had in store for them. They loaded up in cars and trucks, stopping only long enough to buy beer before heading for the creek to celebrate.

Promises to keep in touch got stronger as the night wore on.

"What are your plans?" asked Rose.

"I'm not really sure," Kat replied. "Maybe work for a year and then go to college. How about you?"

"I'm going to become a pharmacist," Rose replied.

"Good! You can sell me Viagra," piped up a fellow from across the campfire.

"From what I've been hearing, you sure don't need any of that stuff," Kat countered.

"Yeah, he needs an endless supply of penicillin, judging by the gals he's been hanging with," yelled one of the other kids.

They bantered and laughed while they drank around the campfire, and finally slept under the stars.

Kat visited with her friends and spent most of the evening dancing.

She was sitting on her chair when a long line of cars drove in.

"Bars closed," someone said. "Hope they brought their own booze."

People staggered to the campfire a few at a time. One young fellow that Kat did not know almost fell in the fire, but was saved just in time by a burly guy who grabbed him as he fell.

Kat's mood changed instantly as she recognized a woman stumbling into the light of the fire. It was her mother.

She stood in the firelight holding a bottle, swaying back and forth to the music, drunk as usual.

Kat quietly slid her chair back into the shadows.

"We should get Skinny hooked up with the Old Cougar," laughed one of the boys beside Kat. "She'd teach him a thing or two."

"Yeah, she's not fussy," said another.

Kat watched in disgust, feeling that her Mother must have no shame at all. She had no business even being here but such was the life of an alcoholic.

Kat's night of celebration was over. She packed up her chair and cooler, and walked through the darkness to her car.

Kat drove slowly to the ranch, embarrassed, mad, sad and confused. How could her own Mother embarrass her like that?

When she got to the driveway, Kat turned off her headlights to drive in by the light of the full moon. She parked and walked slowly across the yard. She was wide awake, so sleep was not an option. A horse nickered from beside the barn, bringing Kat back from her trance. She walked over to scratch the big bay mare that was leaning over the fence.

Kat decided that this would be a great time to go for a ride, so she saddled her up and away they went across the pasture at a gallop. Both Kat and the mare loved the feeling of the wind in their face as they sped along the trails. They rode from the home ranch into the mountain pasture that was open range, where there were no fences for many miles.

They followed the cattle trails until she found the turnoff to Gramps' old line cabin, and followed it until they reached the edge of a high meadow. Kat unsaddled the mare, put her into the corral to graze, and opened the cabin door.

She lit the lantern and fired up the wood in the stove. It was cold up here, but soon the chill was gone and the little shack became warm and cozy. Fatigue won out and Kat crawled into Gramps' sleeping bag and fell asleep.

It was almost noon when Kat finally woke up. A cow moose was grazing contentedly in the meadow in front of the cabin. Songbirds came and went, adding their cheerful sounds to an otherwise silent world.

Kat slipped quietly onto the small veranda just to watch and listen. After a while, the moose had filled up and walked into the bush to lie down. She tried hard not to think about the night before.

Fly fishing had never been one of Kat's talents, but when she spotted the rods hanging on the wall, she decided that this might be the time to give it a try. She took one down and picked up a box of flies before walking down to the creek below the cabin.

Kat fed some line out before she tried to cast as she had watched Gramps do, but when she tried, the fly hooked in the bush behind her. Kat tried over and over before she finally got the fly to lay out in the water in front of her.

Kat knew she should head back but she was enjoying herself. Besides, she thought to herself, nobody really cared.

She heard the horses plodding their way toward her before she finally saw them. Gramps was in the lead, wearing his battered old cowboy hat and chaps, while Gram followed on her old sway backed horse wearing her funny looking gardening hat with a yellow hatband and imitation flowers sticking out. They appeared as they had somehow missed the last fifty years of progress.

Kat waved and ran over to meet them.

"What are you guys doing way out here?" she asked.

"We were worried about you, dear." Gram said. "When we saw that your car was home and your saddle horse was gone, we thought we should check that you were all right. Gramps followed your tracks up here."

"Hop down and I'll make some coffee," Kat said. "I see you've got your bedrolls, so I guess I'm staying another night."

The old-timers slowly dismounted from their saddles, trying not to be too obvious as they headed to the cabin. Kat unsaddled the horses and put them into the corral.

"See you been fishin,'" Gramps said. "Those rods haven't been off the wall since old Thacker and I went fishin' last summer. How'd you make out?"

"I need a lot more practice," was Kat's reply.

"What brings you all the way out here in the middle of the night anyway?" Gram asked.

Kat proceeded to tell her all about the night before, how her mother had shown up at the party and embarrassed her to the point where she had to leave. Gramps and Gram sat quietly listening to every word. Kat kept no secrets from them and held nothing back.

When she was finished, Gram asked, "How could your mother embarrass you when she didn't even know that you were there?"

Kat explained that she was embarrassed by her mother almost every time she saw her. She was drunk more often than not, and knew no shame. To come to a party with Kat's friends was the ultimate disgrace.

"Your mother is an alcoholic, Kat. Most of the time she's drunk and uses poor judgement. You can't change that, no matter how hard you try. She's the only one that can do that, but don't hate her. What she does is never meant to hurt you. She just can't help herself."

"And don't you sit around and feel sorry for yourself either," Gramps said firmly. "That won't do anybody any good. Get out there and do some good and make something of yourself. You'll get a whole lot more satisfaction out of helping somebody else than you will sitting around feeling sorry for yourself."

Gramps could be very persuasive at times, and this was one of those times. Kat knew better than to ever mention it to them again.

Gram had a huge picnic lunch tied to the back of her saddle that she eventually set out on the outside table. They all sat around munching and chatting until they were stuffed. Then each of them found a shady spot on the cool, moist grass, where they could lie down for an afternoon nap.

The sun was beginning to descend when Gramps went into the cabin and brought out an old checkerboard. The tournament that followed was intense, with Gram finally taking the championship.

THE MUSHROOM PICKER

Gramps got out his transistor radio and listened to the news, as he did every night before he went to bed. He always made a point of keeping track of all of the major events that happened around the world.

Kat hopped back into the sleeping bag and Gramps and Gram unrolled their bedrolls onto the other two bunks. Kat was almost asleep when Gramps said goodnight as he reached over and turned out the lantern.

Kat went back to her mother's, and worked every day at Smiley's Burgers. Old Smiley was a nice fellow who barely made enough to pay the bills. He liked what he did though, and the local kids liked him and supported the business. He was always friendly to Kat, and she to him.

Smiley's wife had not learned to speak English very well, so she and Kat rarely talked, but they liked each other. She often cooked something special for Kat and was thrilled when she liked it. The rumor was that she had been a "mail order bride", but nobody around town knew for sure.

One rainy afternoon, when Kat was busy cleaning up from the noon rush, her dad came racing up in his old truck.

He ran into the little coffee shop and yelled "Kat, come with me!"

"What is it, Dad?"

"I'll explain everything on the way," he said anxiously, looking tired and pale.

Kat ran back into the kitchen and called to Smiley, "Something's up so I gotta run."

Smiley looked up and said, "Go ahead, Kat. See you tomorrow."

Kat grabbed her purse and ran out the door to where her father waited. As they pulled onto the highway she repeated, "What's wrong, Dad?"

He looked over to her and said quietly, "Kat, Gramps and Gram were in a bad accident today. They were hit by a logging truck."

"How bad?" she asked, feeling the horror tighten her stomach. Tears emerged, and she began sobbing.

"Bad," Dad said. They drove along, deep in their own thoughts.

As they approached the city Dad said, "Better shape up pretty soon. You know what they'll say if they see you bawling."

Kat recalled Gramps' lecture that she had listened to so many times at the supper table. He used to say, "You gotta be tough to survive in this old world, Kat. Never let anybody push you around and, when things go wrong, don't get all emotional. Use that energy to think and plan, then you fight your way back.

"If your horse bucks you off, what are you supposed to do? The old saying is to dust yourself off and get right back on. My theory is that you pick up a switch and show that horse who's boss. Then you get back on. Forget about the dusting off part. That's only for the movies. Real cowboys are always dusty anyway."

Then Gram would pipe up, "Kat, I think that it's more important for girls to be strong nowadays. I hear about all of those wife beatings and think of what would have happened to anybody around here who had done that when I was a girl. They would have wound up dead. Every man in the neighborhood would have had a piece of that guy.

"I heard of a white man who tried raping a girl on the Indian reserve. When the Indians caught him they castrated him with a sardine can. Served him right.

"Now that's justice. If anything like that had happened to my mother she'd have waited for the opportunity and done it herself. Now there was a true pioneer. You're much like her, Kat."

Kat could not let her emotions show, and knew it. She held her head high as she walked into the hospital with her father. They were escorted into a tiny room and asked to wait there.

Two doctors walked in and one said, very gravely, "I have some very bad news for you both. We did everything we could, but both of your parents have passed away, Mr. Townsend. I think that they both became unconscious upon impact, and neither of them ever regained consciousness."

Kat stood there holding her father's hand, neither of them knowing what to say. They both had their moment of emotion and were now quite composed.

"We need you to come with us and sign some papers," said the older doctor, as he opened the door and led them away.

The rest of the day was just a blur. They had to make certain that Gramps and Gram were properly taken care of.

As they were preparing to leave the hospital a man stepped up to Kat and asked if he could ask a few questions.

Her dad overheard and said, "Who are you, and why do you need to talk to us right now?"

"My name is Myles Schmidt, and I represent Quigley Insurance Brokerage. I need you to sign some papers right away so that we can proceed with the insurance claim and get it settled as soon as possible."

"Whose insurance?" asked Dad.

"We are the insurer of Wilderness Holdings, the owner of the logging truck," the man muttered.

"Then you can beat it," Kat's dad said coolly. "We'll call you if we want to talk to you. Just leave me your business card."

"But you need to sign these papers today," Myles insisted.

With a look that could kill, Dad grabbed the papers from the man's hand, tore them in half, and handed them back with a shove.

Myles knew that, for his own safety, he had to leave. He walked away in disgrace as Kat and her dad watched.

"Would you like to stay over tonight? We have lots to do yet. I have to call your sister and a couple of Gram's friends. They'll spread the word. We have to make funeral arrangements tomorrow. There's probably lots I haven't even thought of."

She would have loved to spend the evening with her father, but knew that she was not welcome at his wife's house. Old Sheila would throw a fit, and Kat was afraid she might say or do something she would regret later. Her dad had been through enough for one day, and did not need to deal with that.

Kat simply said, "No, Dad, I need to go back out to Smiley's and talk to him. I need to find someone to work for me for a couple of days. Could you drive me out there?"

"Glad to, but you really should stay," he said, suspecting the reason why Kat was not staying over.

When they got to Smiley's, Dad said, "Kat, wait in the truck for a minute. I've got to talk to Smiley and then run out to the ranch."

He went in while Kat waited, and was back in a few minutes.

They drove quietly to the ranch, and Dad hopped up on the top rail that was shiny from wear. He studied the cattle for a few minutes and then went and checked that nothing was locked in the barn.

They went to the house and cleaned out the fridge. Sprig was there, waiting, when they took the bowl out to her.

"We may not be back for a few days, so we'd better check everything. The cattle have lots of pasture and water, so they're okay. The haying is about done. Gram got rid of the chickens last year, and the garden's watered."

They drove back to town and Kat jumped out at Smiley's, wanting to stay with her Dad, but wishing him good-bye.

When she walked into the little coffee shop, Mrs. Smiley walked over and hugged her with tears in her eyes.

Smiley came up and gave her a big hug as well. He said, "I'm sorry to hear about your folks, Kat."

Mrs. Smiley sat her down in front of a huge plate of food and Kat realized that she was hungry. She had not eaten for hours, and it was nearly midnight. The days were long in the northern summer.

When she had finished, Smiley said, " Where are you staying tonight?"

"Not sure," she replied.

"Greta and I would be honored if you'd spend the night at our place."

Kat was beginning to feel lonely, so she accepted.

Greta made tea and set out some pastries, smiling often at Kat, but speaking little. When they were finished their tea, Greta pulled out a tattered photo album.

"My family," she said proudly, and opened the album. She pointed to a picture of two young men and said, "My brothers, gone now."

Smiley explained that Greta had had two older brothers who were killed in World War II.

Greta pointed towards a young girl sitting among a bunch of flowers and announced, "Sister. She in England now. She come here to visit a couple times."

She chattered and pointed, with Smiley filling in the details, until they all decided that it was time to turn in.

When Greta opened the door to the guest room, Kat just stood there in awe. The walls of the room were covered in paintings, better than anything she had ever seen.

Kat studied them for a minute and said, "Your sister painted these."

Greta smiled and quietly said, "No, me."

"Why don't you paint for a living?" said Kat.

"No, me cook," was all Greta said, and it was left at that.

They were all up before dawn, and off to open the little café. Kat dreaded the day that awaited her.

The sun was coming up when Dad's old pickup rolled into the parking lot.

When he walked in, he and Smiley exchanged glances, and Kat knew instantly that her stay-over had been arranged the night before. It comforted her to know that folks still cared about her.

Sheila was nowhere to be seen and Kat thought, "You'd think the old bag would at least help Dad out today." Kat swore she would not forget this one.

Smiley was saying, "We sure enjoyed Kat's company last night, Stan. When you're done with the funeral and everything, why don't you just come and stay with us, Kat? We'd sure like to have you, and I can't begin to eat all that Greta cooks. She'd love having another woman to talk to."

Kat said "Thanks, Smiley, I'll do that." She sure did not want to go back to her mother's.

They hopped into the old truck and headed back to Calgary. It was only thirty miles but seemed to take forever.

"I talked to Theresa last night. She doesn't think she can make it here for the funeral, what with the kids and all," Dad said.

Kat's sister Theresa was married to an accountant, who ran his own business in Houston, Texas. They had two boys whom Kat had never seen. Theresa had not been back to Alberta in years, and Kat decided that she must be very content there, with her home and family.

Kat felt very happy for her, and told her dad so. They both knew that Theresa would always have her life in order, and never leave anything to chance.

Kat's brother had also left home early, and had not contacted anyone in the family for over two years. They worried about him, but there was nothing that they could do. Kat always tried to avoid talking about Erik, as she knew that it bothered her dad, but felt that she needed to ask.

"Talked to Erik?"

"No, I don't even know where he lives any more. I sure wish that he'd call but I think that he figures we're mad at him for the way he lives. Gramps and him sure didn't get along. Just too different, I guess."

Kat missed Erik. When they were kids, he was always "Big Brother", there to help her with whatever troubles she encountered. He beat up the bullies when they teased her about her freckles, and helped her out when she got her boots stuck in the mud.

When Erik was a teenager he found that he was different from the other boys. Eventually he chose a gay lifestyle that did not fit in the northern ranch country, so he moved away. Whenever he came back to visit, he and Gramps would argue late into the night. He finally quit calling after their parents split up.

When Kat and her Dad arrived at the funeral home, a surly looking man in a black suit met them and explained that he was a funeral director. He was arrogant and conceited, and Kat took an instant dislike to him.

They ordered handouts and chose the pallbearers. Flowers were ordered and funeral cars arranged for. Gramps and Gram had bought their plots at the local cemetery years ago when the community needed money, so that was already taken care of.

When everything was arranged, the Director gave them a cost estimate and said that they could wait until the estate was settled for payment, but they would have to pay interest. Dad muttered that for what they charge, they were rip-off artists.

They left the funeral home as quickly as they could, and went back to town to visit Reverend Hernandez. He and Gram had been great friends, and not only met in church but visited each other as well.

The Reverend said he would take care of the service, the church and any incidentals. He talked to them for a long while about the meaning of life before they finally left.

"Are we done?" her dad asked Kat as they left the church.

"I think so," she said numbly. Neither of them had ever arranged a funeral before so they were not really sure.

"Better check the ranch," Dad said.

Kat thought for a minute and said, "Can we stop at Smiley's for a minute?"

She ran into the coffee shop and was back in a few moments, carrying a small garbage bag.

"Scraps for Sprig," she said.

They drove into the quiet yard, and both hopped onto the top rail and began to look around.

Sprig spotted them and came rambling toward them. Kat dropped the scraps onto the ground and Sprig sniffed them before grunting her approval. Kat sat on the top rail and watched her.

"Did Gramps ever mention a will, Kat?" Dad asked. "Sheila thinks we need to settle things quickly."

Kat felt her blood pressure rise with anger. She hated Sheila and how she used her dad. Gramps' words rang loudly, "Don't waste your energy on emotion, use it to think and plan."

"No, he never mentioned anything about a will," she said. "That old judge friend of his advised him when he had any legal stuff. Why is Sheila concerned?"

"She thinks that if there is any money, then we can pay off our bills, and she'd like to sell the ranch and buy a big house in the city," Dad said.

Kat was furious but tried to keep her cool.

"Are you sure she isn't using you, Dad? She sure seems to like the good life."

"Don't know, Kat. I know it sure seems that way sometimes, but I married her, so I guess I've made a commitment. I can't keep changing wives every few years."

"Just watch your money, Dad, or she'll break you."

"I will, Kat, and thanks for the advice. Sometimes I just blame myself when her and her family start bitching at me."

When they decided that everything was shipshape, they went back to Smiley's, where they had supper before Dad headed home for the night.

The days before the funeral were a blur. Gramps' and Gram's friends and neighbors stopped in at Smiley's with offers of help. Gramps' old friend Elmer took the saddle horse to his place, promising to take care of it for as long as Kat wanted. The cattle were going to be looked after by the Watson kids until the estate was settled.

The neighbors all got together and built a house and pen for Sprig at

Smiley's. Greta had offered to take her, and a new friendship had begun.

The church was full, and people had to stand on the steps and outside in the yard. Kat sat in the front row with her Dad and his new family.

As they were sitting, waiting while the organ softly played, Jacob pulled an electronic game out of his pocket and started playing it. Dad deftly reached over and grabbed it from him. He glared at Jacob, quietly placed the toy on the floor and ground it to pieces with the heel of his shoe.

There were two coffins at the front of the church, draped in flowers. There were so many flowers that it seemed like a jungle. Kat thought, "Gram sure would have been proud." Gramps would have said, "Waste of good money," but would have been secretly overjoyed.

Reverend Hernandez said prayers and read the eulogy. The congregation sang hymns, there were more prayers, and finally the pallbearers carried the coffins to the waiting hearses.

The graveside service was very short and everyone went back to the community centre to visit. Old friends grouped together to discuss old times which every one of them missed. Their community had gradually broken up, with the pioneer families moving away to make way for executives and recreation lovers, who all preferred their privacy to traditional community.

Kat was the last one to leave. Many people came up to her and tried to console her by saying wonderful things about her Grandparents. Some of the old men simply came up to her and shook her hand. She knew most of the people, but there were many that she may have met but could not remember, or had never met at all. They had come in droves though, to bid her Grandparents a final farewell.

Back at Smiley's, she sat alone in the corner and pondered. What would she do with the rest of her life? She liked it here, but would like to see what the rest of the world was like. Kat could not sit still long enough to have an office job. No special young man had particularly caught her eye yet.

She decided that now was not the time for career decisions so she went and helped Greta with the dishes.

Kat's Dad walked in the following day, right after most of the lunch customers had left.

"Hi, Dad," she called. "Where's the family?"

"Left them at home sleeping. They don't like it out here anyway. Want to run out to the ranch and check things out?"

"Go ahead, and I'll clean up here," said Smiley.

A rabbit was hopping across the yard as they pulled in, and took off when it saw them.

"Wonder where he came from?" they both said at the same time.

They both crawled up onto the top rail and sat quietly, scanning the landscape.

"Hernandez did a good job yesterday," Dad said.

"Yeah, Gram and him were good friends. Gramps and him had friendly arguments about religion and the true meaning of the scriptures."

"Your old Gramps could be a preacher's worst nightmare if they argued with him. He knew a lot about many religions and had his own beliefs. Nobody could change his stubborn old mind," Dad said.

"I didn't know Gramps had been in the American military when he was young," said Kat.

"Yeah, he was a hand to hand combat and survival training officer, but that was before my day."

"That's why he always taught me how to defend myself. He really did know what he was talking about when we used to fight fence posts or willow bushes in the pasture. He'd always tell me, 'Use a club, Kat. Knives are too short and guns run out of bullets.'"

"Yeah, I got the same lectures when I was a kid. I've spent many an afternoon in the pasture fighting willows."

They both laughed. Kat grabbed a stick and started swinging it around.

"I can hear it now. 'Take the pins out from under them. They can't hurt you if they can't walk,'" laughed Dad in Gramps' gruff voice.

Kat whacked the base of the tree with her stick and jumped back up on the corral rail.

After a brief pause, Dad said, "Kat, you must never repeat this, but I think Gramps would want you to know this. You and I are the only ones that know and probably really care anyway.

"When I was a young, a man with a southern drawl would show up at our door every year or so. He and Gramps would go someplace private and talk for hours sometimes. Once I saw them studying maps and making drawings.

"After a couple of days Gramps would pack up his suitcase and say, 'I have to go away for a couple of weeks so you two will have to run the ranch.' I'd ask where he was going and he'd say 'away on business.' He'd come back as brown as if he'd been haying all summer, and skinny as a rail.

"The last time he went out, I was in my early teens. Before he left he called me out to the barn and said, 'Son, this is a tough one and I might not make it back. If I don't, you will have to look after the cows. There will be a man come by and drop off cash every once in a while until I make it home. Don't spend very much in any one place.'

"I asked him where he was going, and he looked at me for a long time before he said, 'To Cambodia, on a mission to retrieve the bodies of some dead American boys not much older than you are, son.'

"That was all he told me. He got back three months later, and always walked with a limp from then on. He never told me what had happened. I had to fight willows and fence posts for months after that."

"Wow, that's quite a story," said Kat. "I'd sure like to know what he didn't tell us. No wonder you and I can fight willows so well."

They both laughed at how silly they must have looked, fighting trees and fence posts with a stick.

Greta and Kat became great friends as the summer wore on. Greta was an excellent artist. She taught Kat about painting and cooking while Kat tutored her in the English language. They both were happy and would chuckle when they made mistakes. Greta would talk to the customers now to test her new skill and was becoming quite the chatterbox. Smiley was proud of both of them and watched over them like an old mother hen.

One morning Kat's mother stopped by the coffee shop. She was alone and was sober for a change. Kat had seen very little of her while she was growing up. She had been a stewardess until she started working in bars so that she could be home more. That's when her serious drinking began. She could be quite a charming woman when she decided to be and when she could stay away from the booze.

"Why don't you come and spend the weekend with me? I'm home alone this weekend and I'm going shopping on Saturday," she proposed.

"Dean's not there?" Kat asked, not wanting anything to do with him.

"No, he's away working," she replied.

"Okay, I'm off this weekend, so I'll come over Friday night." Kat replied happily, hoping that her mother had finally dried out and was sober for good.

On Friday afternoon, Kat headed straight to her mother's place from work. She was tired and wanted nothing better than a Coke and to watch TV until bedtime. When she got there, nobody was home, so she went in to wait for her mom.

She looked in the fridge for a Coke, but there was not a thing in there except some mustard and some dried up old take out food.

"A bit different then Greta's fridge," she thought.

She wandered into the living room, flopped onto the couch, and instantly fell sound asleep.

Kat awoke with a start when she heard the door slam. She looked at her watch and noticed that she had been sleeping for hours. She heard bottles clanging and angry voices. She knew right then that it was a mistake coming here.

Her mother walked in and turned on the living room light. When she saw Kat she gave a snort and said, "Hi, Kat," her eyes struggling to focus.

Dean staggered in with a beer in his hand, and flopped into a chair. When he finally saw Kat he yelled, "What's that little bitch doing in my house?"

"It's not your house. You don't even help pay the rent around here," her mother slurred.

"We share everything around here, don't we, Honey?" Dean said, as he flopped himself onto the couch beside Kat.

"You gonna share your daughter?" he taunted the older woman, as he grabbed at Kat.

She was wide awake now and jerked away in a flash before he caught her.

Her mother yelled, "Get out, you filthy bastard, right now."

Dean just sneered at her and then turned back to Kat. He had an evil gleam of lust on his face.

Kat was in terror, but only for an instant. The things that Gramps had begun to teach her from her earliest memories were all coming back. "Don't waste your energy on emotion. Use that adrenaline against your enemy," he had repeated time after time.

Kat was cool now, with her thoughts collected, as she moved warily around the room to avoid Dean. He was a big, strong man who was in good physical condition. Even though he was drunk he was still extremely quick and agile.

As Kat avoided more and more of his advances, he got angrier. He would catch her by the arm and she would tear herself away. He caught her hard on the shoulder and she flew across the coffee table.

Her mother just stood there, screaming for Dean to stop.

He chased her, grunting like a rabid dog, until he finally caught her by the hair. He flung her this way and that while he tore at her clothes.

Kat had never felt pain and anger like she was feeling right now.

As he dragged her past the entryway toward the bedrooms, she spied a set of golf clubs out of the corner of her eye, and grabbed one. She took a firm grip, knowing instinctively that letting go may cost her her life.

It was hard to get a good swing with the big man dragging her by her hair, but she gave him a good whack on the ankle.

He released his grip a bit and she pulled back as hard as she could. She could feel her hair being torn from her scalp as she broke free.

She took a quick step back and swung the club as hard as she could, hitting him squarely on the jaw. As he clutched for his jaw she landed one on his knee and then his ribs, just the way that Gramps had shown her.

Dean dropped to the floor yelling, "Call the cops, she's killing me."

Kat did not stop swinging at the big man until he was flat on the floor, crying like a baby. Her mother had the phone in her hand when Kat left the house.

She drove away, glad to be alive, but feeling sorry for her mother. Nobody needed to put up with a slob like that.

The final breakfast customers had just left the restaurant the following day when a police car rolled up. Two uniformed officers walked in, and politely asked if they could speak to Kathy Townsend.

Kat replied, "That's me. How may I help you?"

"Kathy, you are being charged with aggravated assault as a result of the fight that you were in last night. We are here to advise you that your trial will be held here at the courthouse at ten o'clock on the morning of August fifteenth."

"What? That jerk attacked me!" Kat exclaimed.

"You'll have your day in court to explain yourself," the younger man said.

"How in the world did a little sprite like you beat the daylights out of that big galoot?" said the older officer. "Are you all right, Kathy? Did he hurt you?"

"Yea, I'm all right, missing a bit of hair and a couple of bruises is all. Why am I being charged?"

"He's pretty badly hurt, got a fractured jaw and a chipped kneecap. We had no idea that it was a kid like you that gave him a whopping like that. When people get broken bones in a fight, we automatically press charges. Good luck in court."

Smiley walked out of the kitchen and said, "What was that all about?"

"Oh, got in a bit of a scrap with my mom's boyfriend last night and now I've got to go to court. I could be on the Jerry Springer show." She laughed.

Her court date was in two weeks, so Kat started on Monday morning to prepare for her defence. Within a few days she had everything organized so she was not too worried.

One afternoon, her dad came out to visit her. When she told him about her episode and the upcoming trial, they were both ready to go work Dean over again.

It took her a long time to calm down. It would not have surprised her a bit to find out later that her dad had gone over and had it out with that idiot. She was glad he had not.

Kat's dad was back a few days later. He asked Kat if she would like to go out to the ranch with him and check on things.

On the way out to the ranch Dad asked, "You all ready for the big court case next week, Kat? You know, I was mad at that piss ant for days. I almost drove out there on Sunday but thought the better of it, what with your trial and all. I'll get my chance to tune him in one of these days. What in the world is wrong with your mother to put up with that? Sounds like you worked him over pretty good though, from what I'm hearing from the neighbors."

"She's an alcoholic, Dad. You wouldn't believe what bad shape she's in. I've never seen her this bad, but there's nothing that you or I can do. Don't worry about her boyfriend. I gave him a couple of whacks that even Gramps would have had to admit were pretty solid."

They hopped up onto the top rail and scanned the ranch for quite a while until Dad broke the silence.

"This place is all yours now, Kat."

She almost fell off the corral. "What?"

"Yeah, Gramps wanted to put my name on the land titles last year, in case they passed on. I told him not to, as my marriage wasn't the greatest and I am close to bankruptcy. Gram came up with the idea of putting your name on instead. That way nobody would have any claim, and it would automatically go to you when they passed on. Gramps and I thought it was a great idea, so that's what they did. Now it's yours."

"No, Dad, it belongs to you. My name is just on the titles," Kat said sternly.

"Let's leave it that way and not tell anybody for now. They had enough money in the bank to cover the funeral expenses and a couple thousand left over," Dad said.

"I never had any idea how much money they had," said Kat. "They never talked about money."

They wandered around the pasture to check on the herd, and when they decided that everything was all right, they headed back to Smiley's for supper.

Kat walked into the courtroom with a file in her hand. At precisely ten o'clock a bailiff stood up and announced loudly, "Court of Queen's Bench is now in session. Case, Crown versus Townsend. Judge Thacker presiding."

Dean and Kat's mother were sitting across from Kat. He had his usual sneer and looked like he was nursing a hangover. She just looked miserable.

The Crown Prosecutor was a middle-aged man with a sour expression.

The door swung open and somebody said, "All rise."

The old judge sat down and everyone in the courtroom followed. He slammed his gavel down hard and said in a voice like thunder, "Court is now in session, case please. May I hear the charges?"

"Crown versus Kathy Townsend, aggravated assault, Your Honor."

The old judge glared over his reading glasses and asked, "Who represents the Crown?"

The Crown Prosecutor stood and stated, "I do, Your Honor. Ron Smith, on behalf of the Crown."

"Who represents the Defendant?" the judge asked.

Kat stood up and said, "I do, Your Honor. Kathy Townsend, Defendant."

"Please sit over there, Miss Townsend. How do you plead?"

"Not guilty, Your Honor."

The Prosecutor stated his case and showed the wounds and the broken jaw before he rested.

Kat called Dean to the witness stand and grilled him like a professional.

"How much did you have to drink that day?" she asked.

"Don't know, but I was pretty loaded," he answered.

"Where do you work?" she asked, followed by a multitude of questions to show Dean's character.

"Odd jobs. I help furniture movers load their trucks," Dean answered.

"For cash?"

"Yes."

"Do you pay taxes?" she asked.

"No," was his answer.

"Have you any prior convictions?"

"Yes."

"How many?"

"Don't know," he answered honestly.

"Eleven, to be exact. Mostly assault and attempted rape. Did you hit anyone prior to being hit?" Kat asked.

Dean knew that he could not match wits with Kat. He was becoming frustrated and yelled, "I don't have to answer that."

"You will answer or I'll have you thrown in jail until you do," Judge Thacker thundered.

"Well, I tried to throw her out of my house."

Kat jumped on that. "Do you pay the rent? No? Then what gives you the right to throw me out?"

"I live there," he said.

"My mother has a dog living there too, and it's more useful than you," Kat said as she sat down.

The prosecutor declined to cross-examine, and was beginning to look embarrassed.

Kat called her next witness, Doctor James Waterford.

"Did you examine me on the night of August third?" Kat asked.

"Yes," he said, as he looked over at the Judge. "Kathy came to the emergency room at the hospital. I checked her injuries. It was clear that she had been beaten by a man with large hands. She was missing hair on her head where it had been pulled out. In my opinion, Your Honor, she was the victim of an assault who was merely defending herself."

"Thank you," Kat said.

"Nothing further," the Crown Prosecutor said, embarrassed for having to even sit through this case. He had not spent any time preparing such a simple case, and now he looked the fool.

"Mr. Dean Lucas," the old judge bellowed, "Approach the bench."

Dean sprang up and stood quaking in front of the judge.

"Mr. Lucas, I am charging you with the assault of Miss Kathy Townsend. Unless I hear a lot of new evidence in your defence, your punishment will be extremely severe. You may say that I'll throw the book at you.

"In our country we do not hurt young women, and we have laws to protect them from people like you. I will also be contacting the tax department in regards to your lack of payment. We all pay our share in this country, Mr. Lucas.

"Now get out of my sight until we have our day in court, Mr. Lucas. The clerk will give you the details."

Everyone in the courtroom was pale and sweating after that explosion. The old judge looked up and said, "Kathy Townsend, approach the bench."

Kat stood up and walked over to face her punishment. "He's a tough old bird," she thought.

Judge Thacker stared at her for what seemed an eternity before he said, "You broke his jaw."

"Yes."

"And cracked his kneecap."

"Yes, Your Honor."

"Gave him all those bruises?"

"Yes, Your Honor."

"Then drove yourself to emergency after he pulled out your hair?"

"Yes, Your Honor."

"Have you any remorse for the beating you gave him?"

"No, Your Honor."

"Good," the old judge said, and the entire courtroom took notice. "Kathy Townsend, I find you not guilty of all charges, but may I give you a piece of advice?"

"Sure," said Kat.

"Next time use a driver," he smiled. "May I see you for a minute in my chambers?"

Kat followed him back to chambers.

Judge Thacker looked a lot less menacing without his robes. He sat down slowly and motioned for Kat to sit.

"Saw that moose the other day," he said, and Kat remembered him instantly. He was Gramps' old hunting partner and friend.

"I was very sorry to hear about your grandparents. They were good folks."

"Yes. I'm sorry I didn't recognize you in the courtroom. I apologize."

"Just as well. That guy has been avoiding the law for too long, but he'll get what he's got coming. I don't have much patience with people like that."

They talked for another hour about this and that until the old judge had to go. Kat went out and met her dad, who had been sitting on the steps waiting for her.

He walked over and stared at her for a bit. "You okay, Kat?"

"Yeah," she said. They looked at each other and laughed.

"That piss ant of your mother's sure picked on the wrong kid, didn't he? If the old judge has his way, he'll hang the guy.

"I remember Gramps talking about a couple of scrapes those two got themselves in when they were hunting. One night they got lost and had to spend the night on a mountain in a blizzard. Another time those two old reprobates got into the rum and ended up burning their tent down and had to come home early. Boy, did Gram tie into them both when she found out," Dad chuckled.

They went for ice cream and laughed at Kat's big day in court until they had to go their respective ways. Kat stopped at the cemetery on her way home with fresh flowers for her grandparents' graves.

Kat was the first one to the little coffee shop in the morning. She stopped to enjoy the smell before she turned the light on. "I sure like it here," she thought. "What would I ever had done without these wonderful people?"

Kat did not have serious thoughts very often but was already into it. Summer was almost over and business would be slowing down. Smiley and Greta would be able to take care of the business themselves. They could not afford to keep staff during the winter but she knew they would not have the heart to lay her off.

She decided that she would start looking for something else right away. She did not want to go for a career job yet. She would probably go to college next fall so she just wanted something that paid well.

Smiley and Greta came in, and Greta headed straight for the kitchen. Pots and pans were banging within seconds. Greta was singing an unknown song. She was in her glory.

As Kat and Smiley were setting the tables, she said, " Smiley, I'll be done here soon."

He looked up from what he was doing and said slowly, "You sure don't have to go on our account, Kat. You can stay on if you want to."

"Thanks, but I need to go out and try some different things. I really need to find out what I want to do or take in college."

"Actually, Kat, I think it would do you good to get away from the area for a while. You've been to the cemetery every day since the funeral. Your Dad and Mother are both adults. They will make their choices with or without you. I agree with you that you need to go see the world, but we're going to miss you. I have a friend in Vancouver who has a janitor company. If you want, I can call him."

"I'm just going to look around for a bit," said Kat.

Alison walked into the restaurant with two guys who were well dressed and polite. Alison and Kat had been friends since elementary school. They had drifted apart during high school, but still liked each other.

Kat was busy when she took their order, so she did not have time to visit. When they finished, everyone was gone, so Kat sat down with them.

"Going to college this fall?" Alison asked.

"No, I'm just going to look around for a year or so, and try and figure out what I want to do."

"Why don't you come with us? We're going out to the coast to pick mushrooms. In Japan they are a delicacy. You pick them on the mountains and there are buyers in town who pay cash for them. Up to two hundred dollars a pound. I've heard of people making a fortune if you can find them."

"When are you leaving?" Kat asked.

"Day after tomorrow, so you'd have to decide right away. We're taking the bus, which takes a few days to get there. Got a motel booked for a week. By then we should have enough money to pay the rent or, if we get lucky, we can still make college. The guys are accepted so they have to be back. I haven't heard yet. We can make twenty or thirty thousand in a week if we get lucky."

"We can take my car if you want," Kat said, her mind suddenly made up.

"Could we fit enough stuff in it?"

They spent all afternoon planning like Boy Scouts. Kat was so excited she could barely contain herself.

Sleep did not come easy. Kat dreamed of climbing high mountains with mushrooms behind every tree. If she made that much money, she would buy a new pickup with chrome wheels and a CD player. No, she would give it to her Dad, but then the woman she despised would get it. Yes, she would buy the truck.

Kat was going away for her very first time. She was so excited that she could barely contain herself. Four people would pretty much fill up her little car, so each person could only bring their clothes. She packed and re-packed, bringing only the essentials.

She checked her bank account and verified that she had $600.00 saved up. "This should be lots to do me until the first big mushroom sale," she supposed.

Kat drove up to the cemetery that evening, just to gather her thoughts. The wild flowers that bloomed each spring adorned the unspoiled landscape, so she carefully picked two bouquets of buttercups and shooting stars to place on Gram's and Gramps' graves. She sat quietly, remembering the happiness she had shared with her grandparents, her worries gradually fading.

The squeal of worn out brakes caught her attention. She watched Gram's old friend, Lil, get out and reach for her cane. Kat ran as fast as she could towards Lil and proceeded to give her a hug. Lil was as strong as an ox and almost took Kat's breath away when she hugged her back.

Lil was a widow who raised her family back in the mountains by working her sawmill and trap line. Her husband had died when she was young and they had had three small children. She decided to stay in the mountains and raise the children alone.

Lil and Gram had been the best of friends, even though they were quite different from each other, with Lil being a lot rougher around the edges. She wore a beat up old cowboy hat and riding boots with her faded blue jeans. The truck she drove looked like it was from the fifties, with no lights that worked and fenders that threatened to fall off at any minute.

Lil was the most kind and generous person that Kat had ever met. She always put everyone else's needs far ahead of her own.

"Needed to get some tires for my truck," Lil said. "Found some used ones

THE MUSHROOM PICKER

at the tire shop that should keep her goin' for a while longer. Seen your car here so thought I'd better stop to see if you were okay. You been lickin' that salt block again? Show me your tongue."

"No, Lil," Kat replied. "I haven't licked the salt block in years. When I started school, the kids made fun of me, so I quit." Kat stuck out her tongue for Lil to inspect.

"That little friend, Amanda, must have taught you to do that. Every time I'd visit your Grandma, she'd check your tongue whenever you'd come into the house. The salt block your Granddad had out for the cattle was blue, so it turned your tongue blue whenever you little buggers would lick it. When your Grandma caught you she'd tan your arse and send you both to bed. Your Granddad would just laugh when he'd catch you.

"One day I was sitting in the kitchen, having tea with your Grandma, when I noticed you little brats licking the salt block along with the big herd bull. She had her back to the window so she did not see a thing. When you kids had enough, you went over and laid down in the shed by the bull. It was a long time before you came in and got your lickin' that day."

"I've grown up a bit since then," Kat laughed. "Amanda and I were a bit of trouble for Gram, I suppose. She's a model now, and travels the world. We had lots of fun though, seems like yesterday. How are you really doing, Lil?"

"I'm getting old, and my body's starting to wear out, Kat. I haven't fired up the sawmill for a few years, just sell firewood now. Your Grandma and I sawed a lot of lumber with that old mill. I'd run the saw and she'd pile the lumber. Nobody works like that today, but I was flat broke with three little kids to feed.

"I didn't have any money to pay your grandma, but she just came over and helped. She kept my kids when I was out on the trap line too. I'd never have been able to stay back in the mountains if it weren't for her. Sometimes when your granddad was gone away on one of his adventures I'd go stay with her and help her with the ranch chores. We'd talk for hours. There was no television in those days."

Lil pulled a pouch of tobacco and some papers from her pocket and rolled herself a smoke, then struck a match on the leg of her jeans. She blew a cloud of smoke into the sky and said to Kat, "What your grandparents had was special. A lot different from the man I was married to."

"I've never heard anything about your husband," Kat said. "What was he like?"

"I didn't have a lot of say in who I married, Kat. My mother died when I was very young. When I was old enough my old man paired me off with that old bastard. I had three children with that bugger, then he died. That was one of the happiest days of my life. He used to beat me and work me like a slave."

Lil lifted her hat and showed Kat a scar that ran the full length of her forehead, then another along her chest and then her ear where a piece was missing.

"If I was ever in that situation again, I'd shoot the bastard the very first day and feed him to the pigs," Lil said. "Don't you ever get yourself into something like that, Kat, and if you do, get the hell out. Do whatever it takes, but get away quick and make darned sure he can't hunt you down."

"How did he die?" Kat asked.

"Cops never did figure it out," Lil replied. "Figured he must have fell into the river above the falls. He'd beaten me and the kids real bad, so I didn't get to town for a few days to report him missing. He'd been to town and had come back drunk, with a bunch of booze. They looked for a long time and then came back in the spring and looked some more. They didn't find his shotgun either," she said, with an almost unnoticeable wink.

"Your granddad must have had some pull with the police, because he took off for a while and when he came back the hunt was called off. I was sneaking around in the bush watching them when he came back. He handed the man in charge a note that he read and threw in the fire, then he called in his men and they all went away. They never did come back. "

"I never knew that," Kat said. "I can't imagine you of all people ever being abused."

"I can't believe it either," the old lady said. "Just don't let it happen to you, Kat."

"How are your kids, Lil?" Kat asked.

She knew that Lil had children but had never met them. They were grown and gone by the time she came to Gram's.

"I haven't heard from any of them in years," Lil replied. "I guess I embarrass them with the way I live. They are what you call yuppies, so the things in my world aren't very important to them, unless they think they can sell something. No, Kat, I'm leaving my place to you, but not until they pack me out feet first.

"I still have a lot of livin' to do yet, though. I've wanted all my life to go see Australia, so I bought my ticket last week. I get that old age pension now, so I'm going to go next month. I want to see one of those kangaroos and see the ocean. Never seen them or been on an airplane. Want to do a little fishing over there and maybe try diving on the Great Barrier Reef."

Kat watched the twinkle in Lil's eye turn into a gleam as she talked about her adventure to come. Kat was very happy for her, and wished Gram could be here to see Lil's happiness at the moment.

Kat and Lil groomed everything around the graves, and only left when they were completely satisfied. They stopped at the gate to wish each other well on their adventures to come. Lil had to get home before dark, or else she would have to tape her flashlight to the front bumper of her truck to see by.

Kat said good-bye to Smiley and a teary good-bye to Greta, even though she kept saying she would be back in a couple of weeks. She tried to call her Dad, but only got Sheila or one of the kids. They said they would get her Dad to call, but they never did.

She stopped by the bar to say good-bye to her Mom, but when she peeked in the door, she and Dean were sitting at a table with some of their drinking buddies, both drunk so they did not even notice her. She backed away and watched the door slowly close. "What a waste," she thought, knowing that if her mother would only quit drinking, she could pull herself back together.

"That's it, I'm ready to hit the road," Kat said happily, to nobody in particular.

Backpacks went in first, as they were essential. They almost filled the back of Kat's car. There was only enough room left for a little bit of food.

The boys hopped in the back, and Alison rode shotgun, as Kat pulled out of Smiley's parking lot. The kids all waved good-bye to friends and family who had brought them.

"You're the navigator," Kat chuckled to Alison. "I've never been west of the Rocky Mountains."

"Okay, just turn west on highway #1 and turn north at Kamloops."

They tuned the radio to an oldies station and instantly turned into Elvis impersonators. They sang along with Diana Ross, the Rolling Stones, Creedence Clearwater Revival and some they did not even know, until they were hoarse.

Jeff and Graham were fairly big boys to be riding in the back of the tiny car, but they did not complain. They told jokes between songs, so there was never a dull moment. They stopped often for everyone to get out and stretch.

Jeff had a new camera with a timer, so he would get everything set up and then run around to join them in a group picture. They were all getting pretty good at this until he decided that they needed a group picture in front of a mountain waterfall with all of them standing on their heads. It took a couple of tries but they finally got it.

"We'll never get there at this rate," Kat laughed, but they were enjoying themselves so nobody really cared.

They stopped at the Banff National Park toll booth, where they split the cost of the park pass. They pulled into the town of Banff, which sits nestled among the high Rocky Mountains.

They were all in awe of the incomparable beauty which lay all around them. The air was cool and crisp, with no smell except the slight scent of the miles of spruce and pine trees that surrounded the town. The mountains looked majestic, covered with trees up their sides all the way to the timberline, above which was only bare rock until the peak of snow which covered the top of each mountain. It looked more like a painting than reality.

"It's hard to believe that I've lived this close and never been here," Kat said.

"I worked out here one summer," said Jeff. "Someday, when we have more time, we should come out here and I'll show you around. There is a lot of stuff that you'd never see around here unless you're shown. Caves and waterfalls, and stuff like that."

"Yeah!" they all said at once.

They decided to spend the night there, even though they had not gone very far. It was so beautiful they just had to enjoy it.

They found a campground where they could spend the night. They put up their tarp and rolled their sleeping bags under it. They walked over to the store at the campground and bought some wieners, beans and Kraft dinner. Graham built a fire and proceeded to cook their supper.

They had managed to squeeze two pots into their packs for cooking. The wieners were roasted on a stick until they were almost black. Food is always better cooked outdoors, and this was one of the best meals any of them had ever eaten.

Graham pulled out his old guitar that rode on the seat between him and Jeff. He was an expert musician, and said he had played in a band with his dad since he was just little. There was not a song that he did not know. It did not seem to matter what they requested, he would play it, and usually sing it as well.

Within the hour, there were people from all over the world around their campfire, as the other campers drifted over to listen to the music. Some had come in motor homes, others had campers and trailers, and many of them were travelling through the park on bicycles. They were a happy bunch, and tried to sing along whenever they could. Sometimes they would get a song going in three or four languages, and would end up cracking up with laughter.

When Kat finally crawled into her sleeping bag, most of them were still around the campfire. "This was the most fun I've had in years," was Kat's last thought before she fell asleep.

Only Kat's nose was sticking out of her sleeping bag in the morning. The air was cold, but it was warm in her bedroll. She really did not want to crawl out, so waited until she heard somebody else stir.

She leaped out of her bedroll and grabbed her pack on the way to the washroom building. The tops of the mountains had been repainted overnight with a fresh covering of snow. There was not time to hang around to admire them in the cold morning air, but it was at least a little warmer in the washrooms.

Alison came running in right behind her, and stood there shivering. They both hopped around for a bit and rubbed themselves to get warm. They stepped in front of the mirror, and laughed until they had tears in their eyes.

"We must look like a couple of fools," Kat laughed.

"Yeah, what are we going to do when it gets cold?" replied Alison.

They looked in the mirror and ridiculed themselves. Kat's red hair stuck out in every direction, and was festooned with twigs that she had collected from sleeping on the ground. If someone did not know her, they would think she was a bag lady, with her wild red hair and Michelin Man clothes.

Jeff and Graham had their camp taken down and neatly packed away when the girls walked out of the washroom, freshly showered and full of energy. Kat checked the oil, kicked all the tires and patted the hood of the car.

They all piled in and were off on the next leg of their adventure. None of them had genuine expectations of getting rich on this trip, but they were all young and prone to dreaming.

"What are you going to buy if you make a bundle?" Kat asked nobody in particular.

Alison was first to answer. "I'm going to Hawaii and live there till my money runs out."

Jeff said, quietly, "I'll put it on my student loan, so I'm not quite so far in debt when I finish university. I'd really like to go back and get my Master's degree after I finish."

Graham thought he would buy a new guitar. He had found one that he really liked, but it was way out of his student starvation budget.

"What would you buy, Kat?"

"I'd get a new black pickup truck, with chrome wheels and a CD player," she laughed. The conversation was light and happy as they drove along.

They stopped for breakfast at a truck stop. Their clothes smelled like campfire smoke, so a few of the other customers gave them an extra stare when they sat down.

The waitress was friendly, and chatted with all the customers as she worked. It seemed like she knew all the truck drivers that were sitting around the big centre table. Kat was amazed at how efficient she was, handling all those customers by herself.

When she came over, Kat mentioned that she was a waitress herself. She was accepted instantly as part of the waitresses' elite group, and was given a guided tour.

The lady asked Kat if she wanted a job, and said she would hire her on the spot. Kat told her that she loved the mountains, and promised to consider it, but explained that she would be gone for a few weeks. If the job were still open, she would probably take it.

The old waitress explained that she owned the place. She could find good cooks, but not waitresses, as they are the ones who deal with the customers, and if customers leave mad they do not come back. She liked the way Kat talked to people, and thought Kat may be the key to her finally getting a day off.

Kat said she would be in touch, as they left.

The mountain air was still cool, but the sun was rising and beginning to warm the land. The small meadows and lakes were blanketed in fog. The fresh snow on the mountain tops gleamed in the morning sun. The icicles that had formed overnight at the tiny waterfall along the road were beginning to melt, and the droplets looked like sparkling diamonds.

Wild animals grazed on the lush grass on the roadsides. Elk and deer, as well as a herd of mountain goats, came within a few feet of the car at times.

The four young people stopped and took pictures wherever they could.

It was great to be enjoying this with the best friends that a person could ever want, Kat thought.

Their attempts to listen to the radio were all in vain. Reception was poor, at best, in the mountains.

Graham finally pried his guitar from between Jeff and himself. He played country, then folk music and, as time dragged on, they all found themselves singing rock and roll.

They stopped at every viewpoint to relieve themselves and try to stretch out their cramped bodies.

They turned north off the Trans Canada highway at Kamloops, headed for Williams Lake. The scenery was all new to Kat, and she noticed all the changes in vegetation coming down from the mountains into the valleys and lower regions. The valleys were lush and green but the higher levels were ripe and brown.

A campsite by the highway looked like exactly what they needed. There were lots of trees, and it looked like the washrooms had showers. A small general store stood at the entrance.

They made camp for the second time. When the tarp was up and the sleeping bags rolled out, they went grocery shopping at the store. There were only a few items in the store, so supper once again consisted of hot dogs and beans. None of them minded though, as it still tasted delicious in the clean air.

After they had cleaned up from supper, Graham began strumming his guitar again. The owner of the campground and his wife strolled over with a fresh pot of coffee and sat down to visit. They listened quietly and did not say too much.

The other campers eventually drifted over with drinks and snacks.

"Where are you kids heading?" asked one old timer.

"We're off to the coast to pick mushrooms," Kat said.

"Lots of kids do that," said a lady.

"What place on the coast are you going to?" She asked.

Graham stopped playing and said, "A little place called Bella Coola. Any of you folks know anything about that place?"

Nobody spoke up until an old fellow said, "Never been there myself, but I've talked to people who've been back there. They tell me there is a bad hill going in, steep as can be."

Graham resumed playing, and everyone began chatting again. Eventually they wandered back to their own campsites, and Kat crawled into her sleeping bag.

The stars were bright and she could see the Big Dipper from where she lay. All was quiet, except for the howls from the coyotes echoing among the hills. Kat loved the sounds of the wilderness and fell asleep quickly.

A scream brought Kat from a sound sleep to total awareness. She looked across and saw that people were sitting up in their sleeping bags.

"What was that?" whispered Alison.

"Don't know," they all said quietly.

Jeff pulled out his flashlight and shone it into the darkness, illuminating hundreds of large flying insects. Suddenly a large bird streaked through the beam of light and screamed. Jeff fell back laughing.

"An owl! I thought that we were going to be murder witnesses."

They all breathed a sigh of relief and went back to sleep.

Mornings were much warmer at the campground than they were in the high Rocky Mountains.

Kat crawled slowly from her bedroll. She yawned and stretched, slowly taking in her surroundings.

The owl sat on top of an old tree that had been struck by lightning. Kat wondered if he was laughing at her.

She walked slowly toward the tree and stood there, watching his head swivel around to stare at her. She finally walked away, with the owl still staring.

She grabbed her pack and headed for the washroom. When she walked in, Alison was just leaving. Kat walked past the mirror and laughed. Her red hair poked out in all different directions, and her face was covered with black smudges from the campfire.

"If you ever get a boyfriend, don't take him camping, Kat," Alison teased. "You'll scare him off in the morning."

Kat laughed and threw a washcloth at her.

The campground owners came over as soon as they began taking their tarp down.

"Come on over when you're done," they said.

They loaded everything back into the car and stopped on their way out. The campground owners had coffee and breakfast ready for them, and invited them to help themselves. They dished up and ate like they were starving.

"We sure enjoyed ourselves last night. There's nothing like campfire songs to a traveller. Everybody that has left this morning has stopped by and mentioned what a good time they had. They said to thank you kids and to wish you well," the man said.

His wife said, "Made you kids some lunch," and handed Jeff a large bag.

The four young adventurers drove north until they arrived at a town called Williams Lake. They watched for a sign that said Bella Coola and headed west.

The area was rugged with deep canyons. Within a short time, they were driving through ranching country, and could watch the cattle grazing on the rough pastures.

They had not gone far when they saw a car with a young woman beside it, looking at a flat tire. When Kat pulled over the boys jumped out and asked if they could change it for her.

"Oh, I'd be so thankful," the woman answered.

They began their task while the girls chatted. The lady said she was on her way to Williams Lake from a little town called Anaheim Lake. She had left that morning, and was only now nearing Williams Lake. They decided that they still had a long way to go.

"Have you ever been to Bella Coola?" asked Kat.

"Yes, we go down there quite often," the lady said.

"Is that where the hill is?" asked Kat.

"Yes, it's well marked, so be sure that you put your car into low gear before you go down. Don't ride your brakes or they'll burn off and you won't be able to stop and you'll go over the edge at one of the switchbacks. Go slow and you'll be fine. If your brakes start to get too hot, find a safe place and pull over for a while and let them cool off. A lot of the hill is single lane, so if you meet somebody, one of you will have to back up. The hill is only about ten miles long, but it's an eighteen percent grade. You drop right off the mountains down to sea level in those ten miles. It sounds a lot worse than it really is."

The boys had the tire changed, so she thanked them before they headed their respective ways.

Kat had heard a lot about the hill, and worried that she should have had her brakes checked before she left, as she drove across a high plateau.

They drove through the occasional tiny village, some with only a General Store. The trees had already been touched by frost, and were ablaze with color. The leaves varied from crimson to deep green.

A forest fire was burning out of control, so Kat pulled over to watch. The huge water bombers would fly low over the fire and dump a cloud of red liquid over the fire, then pull up, bank and fly away. Soon there would be another one who would do the same thing.

A smaller spotter plane buzzed around the entire area, co-ordinating the firefight. The fire would blaze up, then the bombers would drop a load onto it and slow it down. Eventually the bombers got the lead and gradually extinguished the fire. They circled a few more times, and finally flew away.

Kat could not help but wonder how many birds and animals had been burned or chased from their homes by the fire. She started her car and headed west.

Alison studied the map as they traveled. They were amazed at how far apart the tiny settlements were. They bought gas at every stop, as the next one was a long way away and may not have gas.

The local people were very happy where they were, and did not seem to travel very much. They sure were a friendly bunch, Kat thought. Everywhere they stopped, people would take time to come over and introduce themselves. They seemed to all be characters.

Living in a lonely place without any peer pressure must make you into a different individual, Kat thought.

They were getting tired when they pulled up in front of the Anaheim Lake Store. The kids took a vote and it was decided that they would spend the night at Anaheim Lake. It would not take long to get to Bella Coola in the morning.

They all walked into the store to pick out some groceries. On the wall hung the cowboy hats of the local ranchers who had passed away. They studied them one by one, until an old couple came up to them and began a conversation.

"Pretty interesting bunch, those rascals. Those men were the pioneers who made this country. You kids staying around here?" asked the old fellow.

"Yes," said Kat. "We're just going to pick up some groceries and find a place to camp."

"You kids don't be buyin' groceries. Percy shot a young moose last fall and my garden needs taken in. Save us hauling the stuff if you kids would come over and help us eat some of it," the old lady said kindly. "You can sleep in the cabin. It's starting to cool off at nights and it's got a cookstove to keep the chill off."

"Sure," they said, not sure what they were getting themselves into.

"Want us to bring anything?" Kat asked.

"No, we've got more than enough," they answered.

Percy led the way in his pickup truck, with the kids following. They drove for what seemed to be a long time, down a dusty gravel road, until they pulled into a lane leading to a beautiful log house, with a smaller house beside it.

Percy came over and said, "Well, this is where we call home. Come on in. Mae went in to put the coffee on."

Kat looked around quickly and thought the place could be a movie set for a Western. The buildings were made of logs and were in perfect condition. Horses looked over the fence from a small paddock by the house, and cattle were bedded down next to a little creek down below.

A generator sputtered to life from one of the buildings. Percy came out and said, "No power lines out here. We're on our own."

The smell of fresh coffee invited them to the house. Mae had coffee and a snack ready for them when they came in. She told them that supper would be at seven o'clock. She said that they used to guide hunters each fall, but they were just too old to do it any more. Now she became lonely in the fall, so she was happy to have them as guests.

Kat crawled up onto the corral rail, where she watched the animals closely. Percy wandered over and sat on a tall stump that she surmised was his personal lookout post.

"Is your bull lame?" Kat asked, watching him carefully.

"He sure is. Needs some antibiotic and his feet trimmed, but Mae and I can't get him into the corral," said Percy.

"Any of these horses good at handling cattle?" asked Kat.

"Yea, the roan's good, but I'm too old to handle him."

Kat hopped down, saying, "If you've got the tack, I'll saddle him up and bring the bull up."

They went to a shed, where they got a saddle and bridle. Kat caught the roan, got him saddled, and rode into the valley, where she cut the lame bull as well as a cow and calf from the herd. The roan worked well for her and soon she was chasing the animals up the trail.

Percy swung the corral gate open, and Kat chased them in. She cut the cow back out and chased the bull and calf into the working alley. She tied the roan and ran to the alley.

"Calf's got a bad eye," she said.

Percy had a box filled with bottles of medicine, syringes, powders and salves for healing the animals. They cleaned the bull's foot and put salve around it before giving him an injection. They put some powder in the calf's eye. Then they glued a large patch over it to keep the sunlight out until it would fall off in a week or so.

There was no time for idle conversation of distractions as they worked, but when they finished, Percy climbed up onto the top rail of the corral and lit a smoke.

"Where'd you learn to work with livestock like that?" he asked.

"I've lived on a ranch most of my life with my grandparents," Kat said. "Gramps and I were the only cowboys most of the time, so we had to do whatever needed doing."

"Feel like a look around the ranch?" asked Percy.

"Sure, the roan's still saddled. You got another saddle horse?" Kat replied.

They saddled a big bay and rode down to the creek where the cattle still were bedded down. They followed a game trail up a hill to a high plateau until it opened up into a meadow where some deer were grazing.

The fawns were busy trying to catch the flies that buzzed around them. They tried everything to get those troublesome flies. They would bite and kick at the flies, until they became playful and bucked around the meadow like so many broncs at a rodeo.

Finally their mothers had had enough of their antics, and led them back into the trees where the flies were fewer and they could lie down in the shade. Kat loved watching the young wild animals in the spring and so did Percy.

They rode around the ranch, checking the water holes and fences, until Percy suggested that they go back to the house for supper.

They unsaddled the horses and put away the gear. When they turned the horses loose in the paddock, they ran around bucking like wild things.

"Sure glad they didn't do that when we was on them. We'd have been walkin' home, Kat," Percy laughed.

A wonderful smell of home cooking came drifting from the house.

Kat could hear people singing and a guitar strumming. The sun was sinking low in the west, shining with such intensity that the brightly colored trees on the hills seemed to glow. The stream gurgled below the house and Kat could see the circular ripples on the water. A trout had risen to feed on an unsuspecting insect that had mistakenly landed on the water that was backed up by a small beaver dam. Only the soft music and the trickle of the tiny brook that ran through the yard could be heard in an otherwise silent world.

As Kat looked around the ranch, she felt a twinge of homesickness and missed her grandparents. She washed up and went to the house to enjoy Mae's hospitality.

The house was a beehive of activity. Mae had cooked a huge moose roast, with fresh potatoes and vegetables from the garden. She had a chair reserved in the corner, and Alison and Jeff were setting the table under her watchful eyes. When the food was set out, they all sat down with old Percy at the head of the table.

Kat started to reach for her fork when she heard Mae say quietly, "Percy, would you please ask grace tonight?"

Percy said a short prayer and said, "Dig in. Better eat it up or the dog will get it. Mae don't like leftovers."

As they ate, a wolf howled close to the house.

"Darned wolves," Percy said. "Howl a lot, but don't really bother much around here. I think the wolves get blamed for a lot of stuff that they don't kill. A lot of those calves are already dead when the wolves eat them up. "

"Are there lots of them in this area?" asked Graham."

"No, there aren't many left," Mae answered.

They talked for hours, until they all started to nod off, and then headed for bed.

The kids rolled out their bedrolls in the guest cabin. It was all made of huge logs, with a stone fireplace and garden doors opening onto a large veranda. Paintings of waterfalls hung on the walls. Mounted fish and big game animals also adorned the inside of the cabin.

Kat rolled her sleeping bag out on one of the bunks in the loft, and lay for a few minutes collecting her thoughts. The generator in the shed idled and the lights dimmed. It shut down and all went black. It was night time in the wilderness.

Through the loft windows, Kat watched as a flashlight pierced a beam in the darkness to light old Percy's way back to the house.

P ercy was sitting on his stump when Kat walked around the yard in the morning.

"Winter's coming, pretty cold this morning," he remarked. "Bull's already walking better. Need some coffee? Mae's got it cookin'."

"Sure," said Kat.

Mae had poor Graham in the corner playing tunes again when Kat and Percy walked in. Mae and Graham had become very good friends in the short time they had known one another, both sharing a great love of music.

Kat was prepared for Percy's grace in the morning. She had almost embarrassed herself last night by digging in first.

"Not many families give thanks any more," she thought. Mae had made biscuits in the wood stove. Plates were filled with bacon and fried potatoes. When breakfast was done, nobody could have eaten another bite.

"Be careful on the hill," warned Percy.

Mae gave Graham a long hug and whispered something to him. Kat got directions back to the highway and they were off. They drove through the ranch country until they turned west at the highway.

The hill sign was not a flashing beacon, nor a row of huge signs giving all the nasty details. Rather, it was a little yellow sign that proclaimed an eighteen percent grade.

Kat stopped at the first pulloff, and they all got out to stretch. It looked like they were about to drive off a cliff to the valley below. The road ran back and forth right below them; a four thousand foot drop in ten miles.

"Wow," thought Kat. "I hope the brakes hold."

Kat put the little car in first gear and began to idle down the hill, beads of sweat appearing on her forehead. None of her passengers said a word.

The car crept slowly down the hill, with Kat braking once in a while to keep the engine slowed down so it could keep acting as a brake. They drove by a huge cement barrier on which somebody had painted "Detour", with arrows pointing straight ahead over the cliff, as a joke. If somebody could have got through that huge barrier, they would have dropped two thousand feet straight down. They all laughed.

They drove slowly around rocks that had rolled onto the narrow single lane road, hoping they would not meet another vehicle. Half the road had washed away in one spot, leaving a narrow path to hug the cliff. If a wheel dropped into the washout, the car might have gone over the cliff.

The car was beginning to smell of burning brakes. Kat slowed to a crawl and pulled over at the next switchback, so another car could get by. They all got out to stretch.

The view was something like Kat had never seen before. The valley was a deep green with splashes of bright red leaves. The river below was a ribbon of silver, winding its way up the valley. Eagles soared and screamed in the valley below. The road wound back and forth below them. Graham set his camera on a tripod to capture permanent images of the scenic beauty.

Everything was back in the car, and they were preparing to continue down, when Jeff said, "I hear a car coming," so they waited. Two boys and a teenage girl raced around the corner on mountain bikes. "Mom and Dad are coming down behind us," they yelled, as they flew around the switchback. A couple of minutes later, a man and woman in a pickup went by, grinning and waving. Kat proceeded slowly down the hill, going back and forth, to drop thousands of feet toward the Pacific Ocean.

The road gradually levelled out into the valley below. All the travellers breathed a sigh of relief. A sign said they were entering Tweedsmuir Provincial Park.

Kat pulled into a campground, where everyone bailed out and ran around, glad to be alive. They had made it.

None of them had been in the rain forest before and marvelled at the vegetation. Kat and Alison put their arms around the trunk of a tree that was so huge they could not touch each other's fingers.

They left the campground toward Bella Coola, wondering how they would ever get back up that hill. No wonder they did not get any tourists at Bella Coola. One may never get back out of this place, they laughed.

The highway ran down a lush green valley. As they dropped in elevation they began to pass tiny farms with a few cows. They drove through a settlement called Firvale, and then Hagensborg. Finally the number of houses increased a bit. They marvelled at the old log houses that people still lived in and appeared to be in perfect condition.

Bella Coola finally appeared, to mark the end of their journey. It was nestled in a narrow valley between the Bella Coola River and the mountains. The river ended and the ocean began right in the middle of the little town.

They drove to the harbor at the end of town, to look at the boats. Fish processing was a thing of the past, so the harbor held only a few small fishing boats and some private ones. The days of the town making a living from the ocean were long gone.

The Indian Reserve was at the other end of town. They drove past the church and longhouse. Totems stood proudly, defying change to preserve Native beliefs. Kat wished she knew more about the totems. They had carvings of creatures that represented birds, animals and humans.

The motel was beside the Indian Reserve. Kat hoped she would meet some of the local Native people so she could learn more about their culture. Her new surroundings were so much different from anything she had ever known, she felt she was in a different world.

The town had a smell that was unique. It was made up of smoke from smoke houses that were curing the fish so that it would not spoil, cedar smoke from the chimneys of houses, and rotting salmon that had spawned and now lay dead along the banks of the river. This all mixed up with the odor of the ocean. It was the smell of Bella Coola, smelling just like it had every fall for centuries.

The group checked into a motel, which would be their home for at least a week. Their cabin came equipped with cooking facilities, two double beds and a folding cot. They tossed a coin, and it was decided that the girls would share a bed, and the guys would each get their own.

Jeff won the next toss, so Graham got the hide-a-bed.

After their gear was organized, they walked to the Co-op to get supplies. Rice and macaroni were purchased in abundance, with tomato and mushroom soup. Hamburger was kept to a minimum. They were living on a tight budget, so none of them minded a simple, low cost diet.

Kat looked around the hardware-sporting goods department for items she may need for hiking in the mountains. She tried to remember all of the things that Gramps had told her one needed to survive. She bought a small watertight container, Bic lighter, compass, tiny mirror, fire starter blocks and a plastic box to carry it all, including a strap to hang around her neck.

As she was shopping, a store employee came over and asked if she could help with anything.

"I think I've got everything I need, thanks," replied Kat.

"You picking mushrooms?" the lady asked. She was a middle aged Native woman who was extremely well groomed. She looked more suited to a law office than a Co-op store.

Kat chuckled, "We're gonna try, but I've never done it before, so if we find any it will be a bonus."

"People who pick around here are very secretive. If they find anything, they don't tell anybody, because they will probably find more there next year. I've never picked myself, so I can't help you at all," the lady said.

"It's so beautiful around here that I'll be happy just to hike around the rain forest. I've never seen trees so big or moss so deep. Everything that grows seems to be a type of fern," said Kat.

"By the way, my name is Angela. I live over on the reserve with my sons. Stop by some time for coffee, and I'll give you the guided tour of our little village. There's a lot of history in this area."

"I'm Kat, I'm going to take you up on your offer. I'd better get going or I'll be left behind," she said, as she paid for her items

"Have you seen the petroglyphs?" asked Angela

"No, haven't even heard about them," replied Kat. "What are they?"

"Ancient drawings carved into stone. They have been there for thousands of years, the experts tell us. Nobody knows for sure who carved them, or what they mean. You just follow the trail up Thorsen Creek at the edge of town about a mile. It's worth seeing."

"Thanks, I'll be sure to go there," Kat replied as she was leaving.

Supper was a simple meal of macaroni, tomato soup and hamburger mixed together. After the dishes were washed, they gathered at the table to plan their picking strategy.

"What do these mushrooms look like?" asked Kat.

Jeff had done some research so he was their best authority.

"The tops are white, with a scaly white stem. As they mature they turn pale brown on top. The brown ones aren't worth much. Their name is wild pine mushroom. From what I can find, they only grow in pine forests, at the base of the pine trees. There's not much information to be found. There are buying stations here in town if we find any," he told them.

"Maybe we can get another picker to show us the basics," suggested Alison.

"The lady at the Co-op told me that nobody will show you anything, because they want to protect their areas, so I don't think we'll have much luck there," Kat noted.

Graham said that he had seen a sign on a house saying they bought mushrooms, so he would go and check it out.

They decided that the girls would go up the mountains behind the town, and the guys would take the car and go up the highway a few miles before they started looking. They could comb a larger area that way, and if they found any, they would gather and concentrate on that area.

Kat went for a walk around the town before she went to bed. A white dog came up and sniffed her, then followed her wherever she went. She strolled along the river where rotting fish littered the banks. Some of them had been enormous. She walked to the harbor and along the pier. Boats rocked gently, tightening their ropes.

Kat had been raised on the prairies and foothills of the Rocky Mountains. She had never been around boats, so now she checked every one closely. She figured that some were commercial fishing boats, work boats, pleasure boats and sail boats. She quickly realized how little she knew about ocean life.

As she watched, a large boat came in off the ocean. A young girl stood at the bow and guided her dad to their spot at the pier. As soon as the big boat was in position, the little girl jumped down and tied the boat off like a pro. Kat could not help marvel, as the little girl and her dad handled that boat like masters of the sea.

It was beginning to get darker, so Kat headed back. She stopped at a waterfall by the harbor and watched a pool of salmon, trying in vain to make their way upstream.

It was cold and drizzling in the morning. The mushroom pickers sat at the table and watched in silence as they ate cold cereal.

Jeff and Graham headed out with the car, up the valley.

Kat and Alison stopped at the Co-op where they each bought a rain suit and snacks before starting up the mountain in their search. They spaced out about fifty feet apart as they searched the ground. Within an hour, they were tired and cold, but searched the forest in vain for the rest of the day.

They walked back to the motel with aching muscles and sore feet, without a single mushroom. A hot shower helped them to regain their composure.

Jeff and Graham drove in just before dark.

"Any luck?" Kat asked.

"No, we walked all day and didn't see any mushrooms. We stopped at the buying stand and the guy there told us nobody's finding anything yet. He thinks the weather's been too dry," said Graham. "You get any?"

"No, I think the weather's been too dry," she laughed. "Maybe tomorrow."

The following day was a repeat of the previous one, except the rain stopped and the sun came out.

The girls climbed the trail beside Thorsen Creek. They carefully crossed slippery wooden walking bridges across deep gorges. The trail was almost dark from the rain forest that reached high above them. Whenever a gust of wind shook the gigantic trees, a torrent of rain would fall around them. The creek raced over boulders, through a ravine on their left, in a deafening roar.

Images suddenly appeared on the giant dark stones around them. They stood silently, admiring the ancient drawings. On their left was a steep cliff, with the river swirling wildly through a whirlpool a hundred feet below. They studied the drawings for a long time trying to determine what the figures represented.

"Imagine someone standing here, chiselling these figures, thousands of years ago," said Alison.

"They didn't even have metal to make chisels back then," Kat said. "I did a report on Hawaii once, and many of their carvings looked much like these drawings."

Kat walked over to the edge of the area and stood on the cliff overlooking the whirlpool. "I wonder if those people dropped their sacrifices from here into that pool," she said. "Maybe human sacrifices."

"This is eerie. Let's get out of here," shivered Alison.

Kat had a mystical feeling and vowed to return alone, so she could spend more time studying the drawings. She thought she would bring a notepad, so she could copy the drawings and try to identify the artists.

They traversed the mountain laterally, before finally going back to the motel. No mushrooms again today.

When Kat got out of the shower, Alison was sleeping. She slipped out quietly.

Three fishermen had just arrived, and had lawn chairs set up in front of their cabin. She said, "Hi," as she walked by.

The older fellow stood and said, "Howdy, Ma'am, care for a cocktail?"

Kat looked at them carefully before saying, "My mother's an alcoholic and I sure don't want to end up like her, so I don't drink. I would have a Coke."

"Oh my God," the older fellow exclaimed. "Does that mean if I have a whiskey I could wind up like Rob?" looking at the young guy with a grin.

The other grinned and said, "I'm Rob. Just ignore these old guys. I broke them out of the Lodge for a few days to take them fishing. I drive the Handi-bus."

"Don't believe a word he says. We just brought the kid along to teach him how to fish," said the one who had not spoken yet. "By the way, I'm Norm, this is Robert and you've already met Rob."

"Rob's a little touched, but my daughter married him, so we had to bring him along," said Robert. "Would you marry a guy who looked like that? Looks like a beach ball with eyes. And who might you belong to?" he asked politely, looking at Kat as he handed her a Coke.

"Name's Kat. We're out here for a week or so, looking for mushrooms."

"The kind that make you weird?" Rob asked.

"No," Kat replied, "we're looking for pine mushrooms. Apparently they're a delicacy in Japan."

Kat figured Rob was in his twenties and Robert and Norm were in their forties. They had apparently agreed not to discuss anything about their work, but Kat deduced that they all worked for oil companies. She had no idea of their positions.

Robert had a good sense of humor, which got better with each drink. Kat found herself in stitches more often than not, listening to these guys.

Norm was about the same, but had serious moments. Kat would notice him sometimes looking at the mountains, contemplating a private thought. He and Robert had obviously traveled many exciting trails together. One of them would say a couple of meaningless words and they would both laugh like crazy, both understanding their meaning.

Rob was embarrassed much of the time by his partners. They would be laughing at something, while Rob would try to explain to Kat, who sat beside him on the step, what they were talking about. They sat and talked well into the night, while Robert and Norm filled themselves with whiskey and laughed like a couple of schoolgirls.

They exchanged stories about their lives as the night grew late. There was never an unhappy moment, even though none of them had had it easy. Kat liked these guys.

A white dog joined them, sniffing everyone's legs to determine where they had been. They were still talking when Kat went back to her cabin.

It was sunny and cool when Kat woke up. She remembered that she had forgotten her jacket, hanging on a chair in front of the fishermen's cabin. She passed by a mirror as she left and laughed at herself. Her red hair stuck out in every direction. She wore the ancient sweater and sweat pants she had slept in. She slipped on her old runners, and thought, "Nobody's going to see me anyway."

The door slammed when she was almost to her jacket, and out walked Rob.

"Good morning, Kat."

She kept walking and said, "Morning, Rob," looking at the ground. She quickly grabbed her jacket and went straight back to her cabin. She had never been so embarrassed in her life. She was blushing so badly that her face felt hot.

Kat was not a vain person, but Rob was the last person she wanted to meet, looking like a bag lady. She looked at herself in the mirror and laughed out loud. "Don't need to worry about him making a pass at me," she thought.

Kat woke up Alison and the boys, and they dined on cold cereal.

The mountain seemed steeper this morning. Sticks kept scratching and tearing at Kat's clothes. Her raingear was in tatters, but it still protected her from the water that poured from the trees when the wind blew.

The girls walked back and forth, checking under every tree.

"I found one," screamed Alison.

They got down on their hand and knees, checking the mushroom from top to bottom.

"Sure looks right," Kat said. They picked it and headed back to town in high spirits. They knocked on the door of the "WE BUY MUSHROOMS" house and just stood there.

A man came to the door, and Alison handed him the mushroom. He looked it over carefully and smelled it carefully.

"Wrong kind," he said slowly. "Doesn't smell spicy," he added, before walking back in and closing the door.

The girls' hearts sank. Their hopes of having found a picking area were gone. Slowly they turned back toward their cabin. Both were deep in thought, discouraged by the thoughts of all their effort for no reward.

Kat peeled off her wet clothing and had a hot shower.

"I'm sick of this," Alison said, when she emerged.

"Yeah, I sure wish we'd find something," Kat replied. "Maybe the guys got lucky."

Kat put on her jacket to go for a walk by the river below their cabin. "I hate to quit," she thought, as she walked. Her money was running low, and if she did not find mushrooms soon, she would have to go back. Even so, it had been a wonderful trip so far. She had hoped, but had not planned, to make her fortune anyway. She would never have come to this wonderful place if she had not had some reason.

The car was there when she got back to the motel. Jeff and Graham had walked for miles without finding a single mushroom. Graham had talked to a few people who had told him nobody was finding any.

"I think we've been wasting our time," Jeff said. "Talked to a nice old lady at the EZ Mart today, who told me that mushrooms only grow at higher elevations. She said we have to go back around the bottom of the hill."

"Great," said Alison. "I'm getting tired of this, we're not even making lunch money. We'd do better picking bottles."

"Let's give it a couple more days," Graham said. "Our cabin runs out then."

They discussed their situation and agreed to give it two more days.

"We're going to the bar, want to come?" asked Alison after their supper of wieners and rice.

"No," Kat replied. "I'm too tired." Her funds were low and she did not drink, so bars did not have much appeal.

When Kat went back out for a walk, the fishermen were again sitting on the steps and lawn chairs in front of the cabin.

"Evening, Kat, could we interest you in a tall cool Coke?" asked Robert, standing up and giving her a slight bow.

"Sure, just Coke though," Kat replied, as she sat down on the step beside Rob.

She thought he moved away a bit before he asked, "Any luck?"

"No, she replied. "Thought we had found one but it had the wrong smell. It's tough, nobody will tell you anything. Somebody told Jeff today that you have to go back by the hill to find anything."

"Rob hasn't caught any fish either, but that's different. He's got a serious learning disability," Robert stated mischievously.

Norm added, "Does anybody around here sell fish? Rob needs to buy one. Sure can't catch any."

"See what I have to put up with driving the Handi-bus, Kat? These old fellows can't even remember what they had for lunch."

They told stories about places they had been and exciting things they had done. It sounded like Robert and Norm just went back to work long enough to regroup and head out for another adventure. Kat thought that whenever those two got together they would create an adventure.

She found that Robert and Norm each had two grown up girls, and Rob's daughter was just little. Robert had crash-landed a helicopter a few years back, so he walked with a limp.

They talked about their previous trips to Bella Coola. They had first come here shortly after Robert's crash, and their truck had broken down. Robert could barely walk.

They had got a bit excited when they were scavenging spare parts from the wrecks in the dump, and the bears had chased them out. They ended up getting a part from a local gent who had an old station wagon with the same part. There is no parts outlet in Bella Coola.

"What about the time you caught the rapist, Normy?" Robert asked.

"Aw, that was nothin'," Norm replied.

"Tell us," Kat begged.

"Last time we came back, the truck broke down, so we had to stay in Calgary," Robert explained. "When we came out of the bar, there was a girl screaming on the street and a guy grabbing her. Before I could blink, Normy had him laid out on the pavement, begging for mercy. He was shaking his finger at the guy and lecturing him so bad, I didn't know if the guy was going to die from asphyxiation, or get his eye poked out before Normy was finished." Robert laughed.

"Yeah, you were consoling the girl." Norm looked at Kat. "I asked Robert if he needed help, but he said he was a lover, not a fighter,"

"Yeah, you could have been killed if that dude had a gun," Robert said.

"He wasn't fast enough," Norm laughed. "I had rum."

These guys must never be serious, thought Kat.

Rob leaned over to her and whispered, "Robert's a karate black belt and Normy's an old bar room brawler. They get themselves into some bad scrapes sometimes and make it seem like nothing. They just laugh about it."

"Have you guys seen the petroglyphs?" asked Kat.

"No, what are they?" Norm replied. Kat drew them a map and told them what she knew about them.

"Sure, Rob can't fish and I think he's unteachable," said Robert.

"Do you think I could make it up there with the Handi-bus? These old boys are getting pretty feeble," Rob chuckled.

A fellow who had moved into the cabin across the lane strolled over, and Robert stood up to greet him.

"Good evening, would you like a cocktail?"

"No, thanks," he replied, as he sat down on an extra chair. He introduced himself as Richard from Salt Lake City.

"You a Mormon?" Robert asked.

"Yes," Richard replied, "I'm here for the fishing. I had hoped to fish the river, but don't know where to go or what I need."

Rob and Norm explained to him what gear to take and where to fish the river. He and Norm talked business management strategies for a long time. He was getting ready to leave when Robert said, "We have to leave tomorrow, Richard. Could you keep an eye on Kat for us? Just make sure she's okay. We all worry about a girl alone in the mountains. Got daughters of our own, you know."

"I'd be glad to," replied Richard. "That okay with you, Kat?"

"Sure," she said, not used to having anyone concerned about her well-being.

"You got enough money, Kat?" asked Norm.

"Yes," she replied, knowing that she was running low, but not wanting to take charity.

"If you need money, ask Richard. We'll square up with him later. He's got my address. And don't be too shy," said Robert.

Kat was overwhelmed by the kindness and thoughtfulness of the guys. "If I get married, I want to marry a guy just like Rob," she thought.

She headed to her cabin for the night, a bit sad that the fishermen were leaving in the morning. She was sure she would never forget them.

Kat was sound asleep when Graham and Jeff stumbled in. They had had more than enough to drink, and were in good spirits. They had started the night in the bar, and ended up at a house party. Alison had found a boyfriend, and was still there when they left. He was supposed to be bringing her home later.

Jeff had met a guy who was taking a yacht to Vancouver tomorrow, and had offered them to ride along. They could catch a bus back from Vancouver. They could even use the fishing gear for helping the fellow a bit. Only if Kat did not mind would they go, they said.

"Sure, go," Kat said. "If I didn't have my car here, I'd sure be taking the boat out. It would be the chance of a lifetime."

They decided to go out on the boat and began packing their gear. Kat went back to sleep.

Jeff and Graham were up early. They gave Kat their share of the room rent and were off. Alison had not returned yet, so Kat ate her cereal alone.

The morning was foggy and cool. The smell of wood smoke hung heavily over the town. Kat was sitting by a window when a shiny silver truck pulled up and Alison got out. She walked in with a tall fellow.

"Hi Kat, this is Jeremy. He's going out today and I'm going with him, if it's okay with you," said Alison.

"Sure," Kat replied. "You guys go and have a safe trip out. Be careful on the hill."

She did not tell Alison that the guys had already left, because she was sure that Alison would never willingly leave Kat all alone. Kat was not worried. She had always been a loner.

Alison packed her things and paid her share. They hugged good-bye.

Kat was alone. She felt a slight twinge of loneliness, but it was gone in seconds. She packed her things into her car before checking out of the motel. She thought she would stay a couple of more days before she left to find a real job. She would just sleep in her car.

When she went to check out, Kat met Richard on the sidewalk.

"Are you checking out today?" he asked.

"Yeah," Kat said, "I'm going to stay a couple more days, though. I'll just sleep in my car."

"You're welcome to stay in my cabin if you want to," Richard said. "You needn't sleep in your car, or at least use the bathroom and shower."

"I'm okay. It's pretty comfy in the car, but I'll sure take you up on the bathroom offer. A person gets pretty grubby, hiking the mountains all day."

They talked for a while before Richard handed Kat his spare key. Kat checked out and walked slowly to her car. She drove over to the Co-op store and picked up some snacks for lunch.

"How are you kids making out?" came a voice from behind her. When she turned around, there was Angela.

"I haven't found any mushrooms yet, but I've had a chance to hike the rain forest. It's beautiful," said Kat.

She told Angela all about the things she had seen in the mountains, things that most people would never see in a lifetime. Kat eventually told her that the others had left, but carefully skirted the part about sleeping alone in the car.

"Come over for supper," Angela said.

"I might be late back to town," Kat replied, trying not to impose.

Angela would not take "No" for an answer, and gave Kat directions to her house on the reserve.

Kat drove to the bottom of the hill and put on her tattered rain suit. She hiked far up the valley, following a small stream. She would stop once in a while to watch the salmon swimming in the pools and listen to the water. The sound of the mountain streams relaxed her. She was enjoying her time here so much, she had almost forgotten about looking for mushrooms.

In the early afternoon, Kat followed the stream back to the road where her car was parked. She drove slowly back through Firvale and Hagensborg, before finally stopping in front of Cliff Kopas' store. She talked for a while with the ladies that ran the store. The people there were friendly and helpful, as they helped Kat pick out souvenirs for her dad and Smiley and Greta.

They told her that Cliff Kopas had been a pioneer in the valley, and had helped build the area where everyone heeded their neighbors. Kat bought a book about Ralph Edwards, who had raised his family way back up the valley, before there were any roads.

Kat drove back to the motel and knocked on Richards' door. He answered and invited her in. She showered and freshened herself up before going over to Angela's.

Angela had a fresh salmon baking in the oven, when Kat arrived. The smells of salmon with butter and onions, mixed with cedar fragrance and vegetables, made Kat hungry.

"Kat, this is my mother, Iris. Mom, this is Kat," said Angela.

Iris was an old native woman who still wore her hair in braids. Kat sat down beside her on the chesterfield. They became friends immediately, for they both had a love of the wilderness.

Iris had lived her entire life in Bella Coola, except the two years she had spent on the Queen Charlotte Islands, studying medicine under an old medicine man, when she was young. She knew every place Kat described from her mountain travels during the past few days. She told Kat about some of the plants that she used as medicine. Kat thought she would love to spend more time with her; she knew so much.

Angela served a meal that was exquisite. Fresh salmon from the ocean was much better than the frozen stuff Kat had always had.

Angela's children, Charley and Wanda, joined them at the table for supper. Wanda was going to complete junior high school this year. She was very smart and studious. She reminded Kat of her sister Theresa. Charley was twelve and loved to fish. School was not important to him.

Charley and Iris discussed which fish would be coming up the river tomorrow, and what time they would move up out of the ocean, and where they would school. They talked about the tides and how high the river was. These were all factors to be considered for them to pick the perfect spot in the river. This was Iris's way of passing her knowledge down through the generations.

"How long are you staying in the valley, Kat?" asked Iris.

"Well, I think I'm going to have another look at the petroglyphs tomorrow and leave the following day. I had a job offer on the way out here, so I'm going to see if it's still available," Kat replied

They sat for hours and talked about life in Bella Coola. Then Kat made her way back to the motel.

Kat parked her car in the motel parking lot. She lowered her seat back and crawled into her sleeping bag.

The seat was not comfortable, no matter which way Kat lay. She would sleep for a few minutes at time, before waking with a cramp. As the night wore on, the car became cold and humid inside. Kat must have checked her watch a hundred times before the sky began to lighten in the east.

When she finally got out to stretch, Richard was standing at his door, calling to her.

"Come in and warm up. I've got breakfast ready."

Kat walked in, rubbing her eyes. She felt more tired than when she had gone to bed in the car.

"Help yourself to breakfast," Richard said. "I don't drink coffee, so I hope it's okay. If not, feel free to dump it down the sink."

Kat murmured, "Thanks," and sat down. The coffee gradually warmed her up and the stiffness that gripped her body dissipated. Kat was glad that tonight was her last night in her car. Tomorrow she would leave.

"How's fishing going?" asked Kat.

"I'm sure glad I met those fellows the day I arrived. I picked up the hooks that they recommended, and went to their favorite fishing hole on the river. I've caught fish since I started. You should come with me one of these days, Kat," said Richard.

"I'd love to, but I'm going up to the petroglyphs today and leaving tomorrow."

They talked for a while, until Richard went fishing and Kat headed toward the trail leading up to the mountains, toward the petroglyphs.

As Kat was walking out of town, the white dog that had befriended the fishermen started following her. Rob had named him Kokanee, so, for lack of a better name, that is what she called him.

Kokanee was a shorthaired dog, with hair as white as snow. Kat had no idea who owned him or what breed he was. He seemed to have the run of the town and would come and go as he pleased. Today he was going for a walk with Kat.

Kokanee would lag way back until Kat thought he had gone home, but he would eventually race up with his tail wagging. Kat would sit down and pet him for a minute before they resumed their climb. Kokanee would disappear into the trees to explore once again.

Kat stopped at each ravine to see if there were petroglyphs anywhere else on the trail, but could not find any. When she got to the petroglyphs, she stared at them for a long time, trying to figure out what they meant. Some of the figures resembled humans, others looked like birds, fish and possibly bears.

Kat got out her notebook and carefully drew sketches of each figure. She planned to research the drawings when she settled down.

There must be some information in libraries about ancient drawings from different civilizations, she surmised. She felt a need to find out about who had stood at this mystical place thousands of years ago. Why had they carved those figures for the future generations to see? Kat contemplated their meaning for a long time.

The day was still young, so Kat decided to continue up the mountain. She checked the huge stones for further petroglyphs, but did not see any. Kat found herself travelling parallel to a small stream. She found that staying close to the stream was easier, so she followed it upward toward its source. The deadfall across her path also became less as the vegetation changed with the increase in elevation.

Her stiffness was gone now, and she was enjoying her mountain climb.

Kat's plan was to drive as far as she could tomorrow. She knew she should turn back, but decided she would go on up to a clearing. She would be very late getting back to town, but that did not matter. Nobody was waiting for her. She walked quietly toward a ledge, the mountain on her left and a ravine on her right.

She was coming up to a large deadfall when a huge brown creature reared up from behind it, uttering a thundering roar that seemed to shake the mountain.

The giant grizzly bear hopped over the deadfall before she could move, and brought an enormous paw down across her face. Kokanee was there, barking and biting. Everything turned red as blood flowed into her eyes.

Kat turned to run, and felt the claws tearing flesh from her back as the bear cut her open from scalp to buttocks.

She pulled loose and hurled herself toward the bank. As she threw herself over the edge, she saw the bear wheel around and chase the little dog up the mountain.

Kat fell, rolling and bouncing, to the bottom of the ravine. She landed at the bottom with her knees tucked up to her chest, waiting to die.

"Think, Kat. Use the adrenaline to help yourself. Get up. Move. Keep going," she could hear Gramps' voice yelling at her.

Kat tried to stand, and fell face first into the ground. She could not get her legs to work, no matter how hard she tried. She began to crawl on her hands and knees away from where her fall had stopped. She crawled along the ravine until the going got too tough and then turned down toward the bottom of the canyon.

Her mind was racing, trying to plan her escape. The pain was like nothing she had ever felt before. She tried to blank out the pain in her mind so she would not pass out and let the bear have her for lunch.

Her body began to stiffen, making each movement slower and more difficult. At the bottom of the ravine, Kat crawled toward a narrow mountain stream that ran from the glacier above. She dragged her damaged body slowly up to it, and drank sips of the icy water before plunging her face into clean and soothe her wounds.

The pain in her face left as the cool water licked it. Kat rolled and laid with her back in the cold stream for a while until the pain was relieved. She knew she had to wash the smell of blood away, in case the grizzly returned. She crawled down the middle of the stream so the bear would lose her scent, if it decided to trail her.

The rocks scraped her hands and knees, but the freezing water numbed them. When her face or back became too painful, she would immerse the wounds in the cold water. She crawled down the stream for what seemed like hours. The sun was going down when she realized that she would have to spend the night high on the mountain.

Kat found a small moss-covered spot under some high spruce trees for her camp. She found a slim, dead tree, which she lashed between two trees with the laces from her shoes. She cut spruce branches and leaned them against the pole to make a lean-to shelter, careful not to use the middle-blade of Gramps old jackknife. That one had to be kept sharp for castrating the calves, so Kat would not open it for any other purpose, just for Gramps' sake.

She gathered several layers of the thick moss to make a bed. She would crawl right in the pile of fresh moss and it would keep her warm. Under the bottom layer, she carefully placed spruce boughs with the stems down. She crawled slowly around, gathering dry branches to build a fire, with extra for the night.

By the time Kat was finished making her camp, the pain was excruciating. Kat feared she would pass out as she crawled over and lay in the frigid stream. She noticed that the coins had fallen out of her pocket, and picked them out of the stream and stuck them back into her wet front pocket.

Eventually the pain lessened, and Kat crawled to her camp. Shivering, she lit the dry wood, using the lighter from the survival kit hanging around her neck. The fire flickered slowly into a small but roaring blaze.

Kat dried her wet clothes and warmed herself up, before crawling into her bed of moss. It was more comfortable than she had even hoped it would be. Kat lay there, washed in pain, until sleep finally relieved her.

Kat lay in the middle of the circle, with the dancers moving slowly around her. A drum beat a steady rhythm to which they moved. At the head of the circle dance stood a huge grizzly, with a raven perched on its shoulder.

The dancers were all native, naked to the waist, with scars from the grizzly's claws on their face and body. They were both male and female. Among them beautiful silver salmon swam and eagles soared. The grizzly roared, with a voice like thunder, "You are a warrior now."

Kat felt comfortable and safe here. She knew they were her friends, and the mighty bear would protect her. Her pain was gone. She felt like her energy had returned to a greater level than she had ever known.

She watched the people and animals dance slowly around her as though they were sending energy to her. Suddenly the bear roared again, "Go back to the other side."

Kat woke up with a start. She remembered the dream vividly. It was warm in her bed of moss, and the pain in her back was much less. The fire had died down to just a few embers, but Kat was warm enough without it, so she did not get up to put on more wood.

The stars shone like diamonds in the sky from her viewpoint high on the mountain. Kat could see the Big Dipper and the North Star from where she lay. She did not need the stars to navigate by, she just needed to go downward. She watched the stars until she fell asleep, hoping that the bear would not find her and that she would be able to walk when she awoke.

When Richard returned from a great day on the river, it was late and he presumed Kat would be there. He was going to insist that she stay in his cabin tonight. He could not live with himself, sleeping in a warm bed while she suffered in her car, especially when he had two spare beds that were not being used.

Richard cleaned up and made a sandwich. As he sat at the table eating, he noticed the scrap of paper that Kat had left with Angela's address written on it.

As the evening wore on, he became more worried about Kat. He finally jumped into his pickup and drove to Angela's place. When Angela answered the door, Richard politely introduced himself and explained the situation.

"Come in and meet my mother. She'll know what to do. She's lived all her life in these mountains and knows them like the back of her hand," said Angela.

When Richard walked into the living room, Iris and Charley regarded him quietly. He repeated that Kat was not back yet, as she usually was.

"She's probably lost on the mountain," Iris said. "If you get too high and wander off the trail, it's easy to get lost. You get into the valleys that run crosswise along the mountain and can't find your way back down. Charley will have to go get her," she said, with great pride in her grandson.

"What about the police?" asked Richard.

"They likely won't do anything for a couple of days and we don't even know for sure that she didn't catch a ride out on a boat. They'd need a helicopter and there aren't any in town right now. Charley needs to go and have a look around tomorrow. He knows the country up there pretty good," Iris replied.

Iris and Charley were already sitting at the table drawing out the trails, creeks and valleys that lay above the petroglyphs. Richard finally said goodnight, hoping that they were right and Charley would find Kat tomorrow. He studied the Book of Mormon until he finally fell asleep.

Charley got out the backpack that Iris had given him for his birthday. Iris watched carefully as he redid the pack for his rescue mission the next day. She told him exactly what to pack and how to use each item.

Her tutoring of edible plants and animals never ended when she talked to Charley. He carried the knowledge of the old ways from his grandmother. The two of them would sit for hours, Iris telling legends from the past or talking about the animals, plants, medicine, religion or the trails in the area.

They had developed a special bond between them that nothing could ever break. Their mission now was to find Kat, and neither of them had any doubt that they would succeed. Iris secretly hoped that she would be alive. She had seen too many bodies carried down the mountain.

Kat slept off and on throughout the night. Each time she woke up, the memory of her dream was more vivid. It was as though she had really been there. The pain of her wounds slowly ebbed, but her legs would cramp at times. The night finally faded into the grey of dawn. Fortunately for Kat, the sky was clear and there was no sign of rain on the mountain, unusual for the coast at this time of year.

She lay in her cozy bed of moss until the sun came up and melted the chill from the air. The insects were beginning to fly around when Kat rolled out of the moss. She got to her knees for a minute before she pulled herself up and stood on wobbly legs. She took one step and then another, trying to ignore the pain. The more she walked, the better she felt. It was slow and painful, but she would manage.

Kat retrieved her shoelaces from the ridgepole of her shelter and checked that her lighter was in the kit that hung around her neck. She trudged away from her simple camp with a bit of remorse.

There were lots of berries along her trail for her to eat. Kat was glad that Iris had told her which ones were edible. She walked slowly beside the little stream, watching the trail behind her for signs that the bear may be following her.

The ground levelled off, so Kat could make better time, but her heart sank when she walked to the edge of the cliff over which the stream dropped hundreds of feet straight down. She looked over the area below her for a way down, but could not see any trails. Kat sadly turned away from the cliff in search of another way around.

Kat tried to stay in the sun as much as possible. Between the bear and her tumble down the cliff, her clothing above the waist was pretty well gone. Somewhere in that struggle she had shed her backpack.

She followed trails up and down through the many ravines, trying in vain to get back down the mountain. She ate berries when she found them, and stopped to drink often, so she would maintain her strength. Kat knew now that she would have the strength to get back down, and that she would probably have to spend several nights up here.

Charley was up at the crack of dawn. Iris had his breakfast ready, and had given his pack her final inspection.

Angela came from the shower. She had to work today.

Richard arrived, looking worried. He had not slept all night, thinking of Kat alone on the mountain.

Iris told Charley that if he could not make it off the mountain by 5 P.M., he was to light a smoke signal. That way, she would know he was all right and where he was. If he had found Kat, he was to light another at 5:30. Richard was to go to the petroglyphs and wait until 4 P.M. in case Kat and Charley missed each other on the mountain. If Kat happened to come back, Iris would send up a smoke signal from town at 5.P.M., so Charley could come back down.

Richard and Charley headed up the trail to the petroglyphs, looking for signs of Kat. When they got up to the cliffs, they found tracks from her shoes in the soft mud. It had not rained for two days, so they knew she had been there. They found a couple more tracks on the narrow trail leading up the mountain.

Richard stayed behind in the dark rain forest opening, while Charley began climbing up the trail. He traveled slowly upward, checking every trail that branched off, for the tracks and every cliff and ravine for signs. He scanned the sky for ravens that congregate in the area of any dead animal.

At noon, Charley stopped at a viewpoint, where he ate his lunch. He noticed a track in the mud from Kat's shoe, so he knew she had still been going up when she passed by here. He knew she could not have climbed much farther.

Charley climbed toward a high clearing. He started to climb over a deadfall, when he noticed a tiny piece of cloth on a snag behind him, on the edge of the bank. He inspected it carefully, and saw that the color was not faded or the strands weathered, so he knew it was fresh.

On the other side of the deadfall, he found hair from a grizzly. Charley was already becoming an expert tracker, so he quickly put the pieces of the puzzle together. He looked over the bank to see shreds of cloth waving in the wind, where they had been torn from Kat's body. Her backpack lay at the bottom, with its contents strewn about.

Charley raced down the slope, where he carefully inspected the entire scene. He saw that Kat had jumped over the cliff and survived. If the bear had come down after her, it would have eaten the food beside her pack, but the food was untouched. She must have gone into the creek, he thought, as he followed the trail of blood on the rocks. She lost a lot of blood, he worried, as he walked down the stream.

Charley found the camp Kat had built, and gained respect for the red haired girl. She had made a good camp for a white person, he thought, and left it clean and cold.

He followed the stream to the cliff where Kat had been forced to change direction. He found a fresh track, and went quickly in that direction through the ravines. It was getting late and he would have to signal Grandma soon. He figured he would be spending the night on the mountain.

At 4 P.M., Richard left the petroglyphs and headed to Angela's. Iris met him and they drove to an open spot where they could scan the entire mountainside. Iris built a fire ready to start, in case Kat showed up. They sat quietly, watching the mountain, hoping and praying that everything was all right.

Kat moved carefully along, suffering from the gouges the bear's huge claws had left and the bruises from her tumble down the cliff. She tried hard not to become depressed, but was finding it more and more difficult.

She had been checking her back trail at every opportunity. She broke out on a ledge, and was scanning the trail behind her, when she noticed movement in the trees a long way behind her. Her heart hammered until it hurt, as she tried to think of ways to save herself from the huge grizzly. Her mind raced in fear, until she spotted that silly orange toque going through the bush. It was Charley! Nobody else on earth wore a toque like that even when it was warm.

Kat quickly opened the tiny survival kit from around her neck and flashed the reflection of the setting sun towards Charley. A minute later, he stepped into a clearing and waved his arms to let her know he had seen her. She started toward him as fast as her broken body would take her.

Kat walked out of one side of the clearing, as Charley walked out of the other. They walked quickly toward each other until they got close, when Charley suddenly looked down and his eyes locked onto his shoes.

"Hi, Kat," Charley said, still looking at his shoes.

"What's wrong, Charley?" Kat said, worrying that the huge scratches on her face were scaring the boy.

"You're naked. Here, take my jacket," Charley said, embarrassed to see Kat in her predicament, and handing her his warm fleece jacket. Kat looked down and remembered that she was naked to the waist. She put on the fleece jacket and was suddenly tired.

"Thanks, Charley," she said softly.

Charley raced around to gather dry wood, and lit a huge fire. Kat loved the warmth. When it got to a roaring blaze, he threw green boughs on it so it bellowed black smoke into the sky. Then he went over to Kat and checked the scratches on her face. He dug in his pack for some salve that Iris had made, and handed it to Kat.

"Put this on the wounds," he said.

She gently smeared it on her facial wounds and then handed it back to Charley and said, "Would you put some on my back, please?" as she removed the jacket.

Charley had never been so embarrassed in his life. He had never seen a naked woman before, let alone touched one, but he knew he had to help Kat. He slowly and carefully rubbed the salve on to Kat's wounds, trying not to look at her naked back, embarrassed every time he had to. When he finished, she put the coat back on and thanked him.

Charley piled more wood on the fire, and, when it was blazing, he piled more green boughs on it. The black smoke billowed up from the mountain once again. Iris and Richard smiled and hugged each other before racing off to tell Angela that Kat had been found.

Richard took Angela and Iris for supper at the Hagensborg Hotel. Wanda was spending the evening studying at a friend's place.

They talked for a while about life in Bella Coola. Richard was fascinated by the area, and wanted to know everything about life in the coastal town.

The conversation eventually switched to Richard's life. He was a very devout Mormon, whose entire life revolved around his religion. He talked lovingly about Joseph Smith and Brigham Young, the Mormon Temple and Tabernacle, the history of the Mormons, and how they came to Utah.

Iris was thrilled when he told her of how the crickets were eating the crops of the settlers, and that they expected to starve that winter. A miracle happened when the seagulls came and ate the crickets to save the crops. From that day forward, the seagulls have been praised.

Iris, who loved legends, said she would be sure to relay this one to Charley, when he got down from the mountain. Charley and Kat were always on their minds, so they were a bit preoccupied throughout the evening. They would be happier when the kids were back.

Charley found a ridgepole and lashed it to some trees beside the tiny spring. They cut spruce boughs to make the roof of their shelter, over which Charley laid a sheet of plastic from his pack. They cut soft boughs and laid them with the stems down to sleep on.

Charley gathered a huge pile of wood for the fire. He disappeared into the bush for a short time, returning with two partridges, bagged with his slingshot and cleaned at a waterfall, where he had pitched the remains over the cliff. He roasted them over the campfire with wild onion and butter.

Kat was famished and ate a whole bird by herself. Charley ate the other one. He threw the bones over the cliff when they finished. He had brought two polar fleece bedrolls with space blankets, which he made into two beds.

Kat and Charley crawled into their bedrolls at dusk. Kat was tired, but thankful that Charley had brought the medicine that Iris had made. It soothed her wounds and as she felt more comfortable, she found she could move and rest.

"How bad do you hurt, Kat?" asked Charley.

"Quite a bit, Charley. I got banged up pretty good on my fall, so my legs are bruised. The bear scratches don't hurt nearly as much as they did last night. Thanks for coming to find me."

"Were you scared last night here by yourself?" asked Charley.

"You know, it's strange. I was scared until I had a dream when I fell asleep the first time. After that I had no fear at all," Kat replied.

She told him all about the dream and how she could remember it so vividly. She had never remembered a dream like that.

"You were on the other side," said Charley with authority.

"What's the other side?" asked Kat.

"When us Indians die, we go to the other side, Kat, like Christians go to Heaven. Some people take the form of animals, and some go back and forth. We call them angels in church, but Indian angels sometimes come back as animals. My grandma knows more than I do about it, you should ask her," answered Charley.

They talked for a while about their religious beliefs, both confused and full of questions.

"You got parents, Kat?" asked Charley.

"Yeah, but they're divorced and both have new partners that I can't stand. My mom's an alcoholic. How about your dad, Charley?"

"My dad was a fisherman. He used to go out whenever the quota was open for a week or two, on the fishing boat, you know? They used to dock in Vancouver between quotas.

"One summer, my dad started drinking and quit fishing. He got a job in Vancouver, so we moved there. My mom tried to make him stop but he just got worse. He started using hard drugs, and one day he didn't come home. My mom checked the streets for months looking for him, but finally we had to move back to Bella Coola.

"We think he died, but I keep hoping he'll come back sober, and we can go roaming the mountains together. Is that a silly dream, Kat?"

"No," she said, thinking that the poor boy had too much responsibility for his age.

Charley crawled out and put more wood on the fire. He was wide awake again when he got back into his bedroll. Kat was warm and comfortable in the shelter, with heat radiating from the fire. She felt safe with Charley there to protect her.

When Kat awoke in the morning, the mountain was blanketed with heavy fog. She smelled the ocean in the air. Charley had filled his canvas bucket with water from the spring, and was roasting partridges over the fire, slowly turning them on a stick.

"Morning, Charley," she said. "Looks like you've been busy."

"Yeah, I couldn't sleep, so I got us some partridges for breakfast. Grandma packed us some more food, but we might as well save it for lunch. The water's warm so you can wash your wounds," he said, handing her a small bar of soap.

She knew it was very important to keep them clean so she would not get infection. She washed her face carefully, but could not manage her back by herself. She went behind the shelter and put the jacket on backwards. When she came back, she asked, "Charley, could you wash my back and put the salve on it?"

Charley stared at his feet and said, "Okay," blushing. He tenderly washed her back and smeared salve on the wounds.

"You should leave your coat like that if you're not too cold. Let the fresh air heal those wounds, Kat. They will heal quicker."

"Good idea, Charley. It feels better with nothing rubbing my back," she said.

They took down their camp and put the fire out. The two young adventurers headed back down the mountain to where they were being missed.

Shortly after they left their camp, the rain started. They huddled under a huge tree, bundled up in warm clothes. Charley took out the plastic that had covered their shelter last night and cut it into two long ponchos. He also made a rain hat for Kat with a long tail to keep the cold rain from running down her back. He wore his orange toque as usual.

Richard parked his truck as far up the petroglyph trail as possible. He and Angela hiked the rest of the way and waited in the clearing. Iris had assured them that Charley would come down that particular trail.

When it started to rain, they sat under a huge tree and talked. They both liked Kat very much, and knew that she did not really have a home to go to. They made a pact to help her out until she got settled. Angela had no money and Richard lived far away, but they would do their best.

The rocks on the trail were slippery with the morning's moisture, so each step had to be taken with care. Kat was thankful that Iris had sent her up some extra socks.

Charley stopped under a tree. Looking at Kat, he asked, "How are you doing, Kat? Should we stop for a while?"

"I'm okay," she replied. "I just don't have much stamina any more. Let's stop just for a few minutes. Would you please put some more of your Grandma's salve on my back? It takes away the pain, so I can travel faster."

Charley's eyes avoided Kat's bare skin as he applied the salve with its strong scent of pine and garlic. When he finished, they each had a granola bar from Charley's pack and a long drink of water, and pressed on.

Angela ran over to Charley and hugged him so hard that she lifted him off the ground. He was embarrassed at being hugged by his mother, especially in front of Kat. He was beginning to consider himself a man.

Kat backed up when Angela ran over to hug her. Angela stopped and looked clearly at Kat for the first time. She saw the gouges that the huge bear had made across Kat's pretty, freckled face. She quietly asked Kat if she was all right. She decided to wait until the time was right, to find out exactly what had happened.

The four friends walked down the mountain to where Richard's truck was parked. Charley and Angela hopped into the back while Richard drove Kat back to Angela's.

Iris met them in the driveway and helped Kat out of the truck. She asked simply, "Bear?" as they walked toward the house.

"Yes," Kat replied.

"Big grizzly. Can tell by the claws," Iris replied wisely.

"Would you run over and see if Dr. Singh will come over and have a look at Kat's wounds?" Angela asked Richard and Charley. They were gone in a flash, eager to help.

Iris helped Kat to undress and shower. She found a light, loose fitting bathrobe that would not hurt her wounds. Kat lay on the bed while Iris inspected her from head to toe. She checked each bruise on Kat's legs, checked for broken bones and looked carefully at the cuts on her face and back from the huge bear's claws.

"You'll live, but it's going to be sore for quite a while. Sure must have scared you up on the mountain by yourself, that first night."

"The salve you sent really helps the pain," replied Kat. She added, "I was really scared the first night, and had a strange dream with dancers and animals. I was lying in the middle while they danced around me. The grizzly was at my head, with a raven perched on his shoulder. When I woke up, I wasn't scared any more, and haven't been scared since."

Iris stepped back to stare at Kat for a long time. "You were on the other side, Kat," she said. "The bear marked you."

She asked Kat every detail of her dream, which Kat remembered vividly. She did not say anything, except to ask questions and listen intently to the replies. When Kat finished, Iris said, "When you are better, you must meet with the elders."

Charley burst through the door, with Dr. Singh and a nurse close behind him. Charley had already explained Kat's situation to them, so they followed Iris into the bedroom where Kat lay. They took their turn to check Kat from head to toe.

Dr Singh wiped some of the salve off Kat's back and sniffed it, then smiled at Iris. He checked Kat's joints and bones, before looking up and remarking, "You have no broken bones, young lady. It appears that the ointment that Iris is giving you is working as well as anything I could prescribe. You just need lots of rest."

They left Kat's room so she could rest. Angela had made a pot of tea, so they sat at the kitchen table.

"Would you teach me how the natives treat their ill?" Dr. Singh asked Iris.

"I am getting old and can't travel the mountains to find the medicines like I used to, but I'll teach you what I can," Iris replied.

"We still have much to learn in the field of medicine," said the doctor. "We are continuing to find medicines that native civilizations have known for hundreds of years. Many of the plants from which the medicines are made are becoming extinct, so we need to do our best to protect them. Many of the plants that grow in this rain forest are unique to this region."

Dr. Singh was a kind man who was well liked by the people in the valley. He had come to Bella Coola seven years ago, with the intention of staying only until a position in one of the major cities became available. He kept postponing his moves, until one day he decided he would stay. His family liked the area, and they had forged close friendships. They enjoyed nature and the native culture, so he could envision no place where they could be happier. They had put down roots and made Bella Coola their home.

"How long do you think it will be before Kat can leave?" asked Angela.

"I don't think she should sit in a car for any length of time, for at least a month. The wounds on her back could become infected. They are deep, and will take quite a long time to heal," Dr. Singh replied. "Does she have a place to stay?"

"Of course she will stay here," Angela said. "We have lots of room and between us we can keep a close eye on her."

Richard laid a pile of hundred dollar bills on the table and said, "This should cover her expenses."

Angela looked at the money and said, "We don't need that. We're okay."

"No, I know you could use it and this will help," Richard said as he placed the money in Angela's hand. "Good-night," he said, as he got up to leave.

Dr. Singh and the nurse followed him out.

Kat was so tired that she slept for hours. Iris watched over her as much as she could. When Kat awoke in pain she would clean her wounds and cover them with a fresh layer of salve.

Charley would come in whenever he could, to check on her condition. He would tell Kat and Iris about the places he had been that day.

He liked to travel up and down the river alone, with his fishing rod and slingshot, avoiding the black bears that were feasting on the salmon in the river. The Coho salmon were coming up the river from the ocean to spawn, and Charley usually caught one every time he went out, so the family would have a good supply for winter. He would tell Iris and Kat about how and where each fish hit his hook. He would talk about the eagles and bear he had seen that day.

Kat and Iris waited for his reports and listened intently. Wanda would stop in when she could to check on Kat. She was quiet and shy, but she and Kat were gradually becoming good friends.

Angela came into her room on the second evening, carrying an armload of laundry, and said," How are you doing, Kat? The pain going away?"

"I'm doing well, but the wounds are healing and it stings when I move. I sure hope it gets better in time."

Iris brought her coffee and fresh biscuits before sitting down. "How are you feeling today, Kat?" she asked.

"I'm on the mend, I think," she said. "The bruises look bad, but I guess that's normal."

"Yes," Iris replied. "Do you think you could walk down and meet the elders today?"

"Sure," replied Kat. "I'll just leave a little early because I'm not very speedy."

"I'm not either," said Iris. "Old age is sneaking up on me."

Kat was not sure what was expected of her, but she wanted to learn more about native customs. She cleaned up and Iris dressed her wounds before they left.

Kat and Iris walked very slowly down the street. Kat was happy just to be outdoors, and enjoyed the Bella Coola morning smell, as she called it.

They stopped to admire the totems as they went by. Kat looked much differently at the totems than she had before. The animals from her dream were all there, looking at her in great stature. The bear, the eagle, the raven and the salmon all looked back at her. It was an emotional experience that overwhelmed Kat.

Iris looked at her and held her hand. "You are beginning to understand," was all she said.

They entered the long house through the opening at the bottom of the great Totem. A group of old people sat quietly, staring at them in the darkened room. The nurse that had helped Dr. Singh examine Kat came over and said, "Hello, Kat. You look much better. Let me introduce these people. They are the elders of our tribe. By the way, I'm Shirley."

Standing by each person in turn, she introduced them. "This is Iris, Judy, Delvin, Terry, Roland and Dorothy. They would like to hear about your experiences on the mountain. Please try not to leave out any detail. It may be very important."

Kat felt that she might have descended centuries back in time, had these people only been dressed differently. She did not completely understand why she was here, but she felt she liked them, even though none of them had spoken a single word. She knew that Indians did not speak very much, and when they did it was usually important.

She began with her walk up the trail to the petroglyphs, her lunch, the walk beside the stream and up the ledge. When she got to the part about the bear attack, she could see them listening with intensity.

It was then that they began to ask questions. Kat remembered many things that she had forgotten. When she got to the part about the dream, the questions intensified. This is like being on the witness stand, she thought. These old people should be lawyers.

She described each dancer in detail for them: the bear, raven, eagle and salmon. She described how she had made her way down the mountain, lain in the tiny stream to relieve the pain and clean the wounds, crawled down the stream to break her scent trail. She explained how she had made her shelter, using her shoe laces, and told of all the things she carried in her survival kit.

Kat told them about the survival training that her grandfather had given her, and how he had taught her hand to hand combat from the time she was a small child. He would never end a lesson until she had it perfect.

She told them how Charley had found her and their trip back to town. She talked about the salve that Iris had made, and how well it treated her wounds.

When she finished, the elders sat quietly once again. Shirley served them all hot tea while the elders contemplated the amazing story they had just heard.

Delvin was first to speak. "The bear gave you the mark of the warrior. You are a warrior now."

Roland spoke next. "The bear didn't mean to harm you. He only gave you the mark."

Terry said, "Our people have been given warriors before."

Iris looked up slowly, saying, "You are a warrior now. You will learn what a warrior is. By the time you grow old like us, you will understand, so you can teach the children."

Dorothy spoke very quietly, so they had to strain to hear her. "You were on the other side, Kat. The bear has chosen you. You belong to our tribe now. I welcome you to our tribe.

"You will need to learn our ways, but we will teach you. What you have to do first is to go travel around, and then come back and teach our people the things they need to know. You will learn to become a great warrior in your travels, because other people may see the mark as weakness, rather than your great power. You have fought the great grizzly, which can kill any man."

Kat was very honored, but had to be realistic. "I'm not even an Indian. I've got red hair and freckles," she said.

Delvin replied, "We didn't decide, the great bear did. Being an Indian has nothing to do with the color of your skin. It's the way you live and how you understand nature. It's not a religion either. Many of us belong to different religions, and still believe in the old ways. We honor the things that give us life. And besides," he chuckled, "I've seen some pretty watered down Indians. White man has been here for many generations. You're the first one with freckles, though."

The elders all laughed. They all had a great sense of humor.

"But I'm a girl, and girls aren't usually warriors," Kat said.

Judy got up and sat down close to Kat, saying, "Let me tell you a legend about a warrior girl from long ago, Kat. No white man has ever heard what you are about to hear. You are an Indian now so I can tell you.

"Many years ago, the first sailing ship full of white men came up the channel into our harbor. Our people had never seen a ship like that, so they came to the shore of the ocean to look. White men came in their boats, and our people gave them smoked salmon and berries, as was our tradition of welcoming. They came every day, and we gave them food.

"One day, the young girls were bathing at the waterfall when the white men sneaked up and kidnapped four of them. They took them back to the ship and fired the cannons at the shore, so our braves couldn't go out until after dark to rescue them.

"One of our girls was a warrior just like you, Kat. She had the mark of the grizzly across her face, the same as you have. They tied the other three girls to the rail of the ship, so if the braves came and fired their arrows they may hit the girls, so the braves wouldn't come. They took the warrior and tied her to the captain's bed, and intended to come back and abuse her. They all went to the galley to get drunk and eat before they had their way with the girls.

"As soon as they left the captain's cabin, the warrior escaped. She had arrowheads braided into the long braids in her hair, which she used to cut the ropes. The warrior sneaked out and strangled the man on watch with the rope that had bound her. Then she used it to tie the galley door shut so the crew couldn't get out. She took the dagger from the dead man's belt and cut the other girls loose. That dagger is still with her family right here in Bella Coola.

"The crew had been mending the sails, so there was sailcloth spread all over the deck. The girls tucked the cloth into every corner. Warrior found oil that the sailors used for their lamps, and poured it over the cloth. She took the lighted lamp and ran all over the ship, lighting the cloth. Then the girls jumped into the ocean and swam to shore.

"The entire village came to the shore to watch the big ship burn. Some of the crew got to shore, and our people captured them and used them as slaves for the rest of their lives. The ship sank right out there in the harbor. The mast still stuck out of the water when I was a little girl. The birds used to land on it. White man never knew that was the top of a mast sticking out and nobody ever told them.

"You have the mark now, Kat, so you will be a warrior whether you want to or not. You have been to the other side, which most of us have never been, and won't see until we return to the Creator."

Roland looked up and said, "One time my son went missing on a hunting trip. I looked for days on the mountain where he was hunting. One night the eagle came to me in my dream and said, 'I will show you the way.' The next day when I was looking, I saw a huge eagle circling on the other side of the river. I knew the boy had been hunting on this side, but I didn't know that he had crossed the river.

"When I looked under where the eagle hovered, there was my son, holed up in a cave, hurt but alive. A bank had given away when he had been walking along the river, and he got washed in. He grabbed a tree and was carried across. Always listen to the messages from the other side, Kat."

Shirley served more tea and some lunch. Kat found she was hungry. She had no idea what time it was. While they had lunch, the elders took turn visiting with her. They would check her wounds carefully and talk to her about her dream.

They were all quiet, friendly people who loved their village and their culture. They were all especially concerned about the young people. There were so many modern places that appeared much more appealing to the young people. They played Nintendo instead of fishing. Then there were drugs and alcohol. They could go on forever about the damage they had done to their people.

The village definitely had a dark side, and Kat was now expected to help clean it up. She was the Warrior.

Kat's head was spinning by the time she and Iris finally left. "What happened in there?" she asked Iris.

"The elders interpreted your dream for you," she replied. "You've found your calling, Kat. What you have to do now is to go look around the world, and then come back and help these people. Their world is gradually falling apart, and they don't know what to do about it. Do they just become white men, or try to keep their traditions? That's where you come in, Kat."

Kat was hobbling down the street when a small white dog came racing around the corner. He ran over to Kat and sniffed her, licked her hand and was gone in a flash to finish his rounds. It was Kokanee! Kat was thrilled to see that the little dog had survived, and appeared to be unscathed.

She said, "That's the dog that was up the mountain with me, Iris." Iris watched the dog run into every driveway and sniff at everything he passed. He barked at a cat that teased him from behind a window and raced away.

"That is the busiest dog I have ever seen," Iris said. "He checks out everything in the entire valley every few hours. He lives where he feels like that day, moves around a lot."

Kat laughed and said, "He moved in with some fishermen that were at the motel. He'd just come in at night and wouldn't leave. Then he'd take off in the morning. Rob named him Kokanee."

"That kind of suits him," Iris said.

They stopped at the Co-op where Angela was working. Kat went over and looked at the fishing gear while Iris and Angela talked. She wondered why there were so many different types of fishhooks.

"Can I help you find something, Kat?" asked Angela from behind her.

"No, I was just looking at the hooks. There are so many kinds, I wouldn't know what to use. I'd like to learn to fish someday."

"Why don't you get Charley to teach you, Kat? He goes every day. The fresh air would be good for you, and it would be good for Charley to have somebody to talk to as well. There's a lot of gear at the house, so you don't need to buy anything. I can talk to Charley if you want," said Angela.

"No, that's fine," replied Kat. "I'll ask him. I need the exercise so that I heal up quick. "

Kat and Iris walked over to Cliff Kopas' store to see if they had anything new. Kat loved the smell in the store. They sold beaded buckskin medicine pouches made by the local natives. They had a faint smell of smoke. There were cedar boxes and carvings. There were perfumes and candles that added to the aroma. Kat thought that, if she were blindfolded, she would be able to tell where she was in Cliff Kopas' store. They visited for a while before heading home.

When Charley arrived home, Kat asked him if he would teach her how to fish. "Sure," he said. "Let's see if we can find you some stuff."

Charley went into an old shed back of the house, with Kat slowly following. He took a rod down from the wall and found a reel stored neatly in a wooden box. He picked up a small tackle box and they went into the house, packing the gear.

When they had everything cleaned up, they headed for the river. It was getting late, so Kat's first lesson would have to be short. As they walked, Charley explained what everything was and how to use it.

"How do you know what hook to use?" asked Kat.

Charley replied, "It depends on how dirty the water is, how high the water is, what fish are in the river and a thousand other things."

Kat thought she would never learn how to fish. She laughed and thought of Rob. She wondered how his trip home had been, driving the Handi-bus with that pair of jokers he was with.

"I have a trick though, Kat," Charley said, grinning. "I just ask my mom. She sells the hooks to the fishermen, so she always knows what the fish are biting." They both laughed hysterically.

When they got to the river, Charley found a long gravel bar to stand on for Kat to learn to cast. She tangled her line in the reel time after time, but, when the lesson was over, she was getting better. They laughed and giggled all the way home, with Kat hobbling painfully along.

As the days went by, Kat's wounds slowly began to heal. Her fishing skills also improved. One evening Charley said, "Kat, you're ready to catch a salmon. Let's go to the fishing hole today." Kat was thrilled.

Charley showed her where to stand and exactly the spot to cast into. "You have to feel the river through the line, Kat. Let the hook drop but not deep enough to snag. Let it tick on the bottom. When you feel it in the channel, let out the line, but don't snag on the bottom. Don't get a belly in the line."

Kat thought Charley was a great teacher, but what a perfectionist! The rod jumped, and just about tore out of her hand. A big silver fish rose high above the river, and landed with a splash.

"Keep the rod tip up! Let out some line! Reel!" Charley shouted, as Kat fought the fish to shore. She slowly worked it to the bank, until Charley grabbed it and killed it before holding it high.

"Supper," he said. "Your first fish will be supper tonight."

Kat had mixed emotions as Charley cleaned the sleek Coho salmon. She was proud that she was supplying food for the family, but sad to see the fish die. They talked about it on the way back.

"No hunter likes to watch an animal die, Kat, but they give us our food. Hunters protect the animals so they don't die needlessly," said Charley.

"Yes, I understand now," said Kat. "I guess it's the same as ranchers. They treat their animals as well as they can. They help them when they're born, and treat them when they are sick, even though they will become food for people. Thanks for teaching me how to fish, Charley."

Charley looked toward Kat for a minute, and then asked her, "What can you teach me, Kat?"

"Well, Charley," Kat said, "I could teach you how to be a waitress or a cook."

"Yuck," said Charley.

Kat continued, "I could teach you how to drive, but you're too young. Wait - I could teach you how to fight with a club. My grandfather used to teach me every day we were together, for years."

"Sure," Charley said, "I'd like to learn how in case I need to fight sometime."

"Okay," said Kat, "but you'll have to promise me that you'll only use what I teach you in self-defence."

"Sure," answered Charley, "I promise. I'm not a bully, and I hate bullies."

When they got home, Iris and Angela congratulated Kat and shook her hand for catching her first salmon. It was a milestone around their house. Iris washed and baked the salmon. Kat laughed at herself for thinking it was the best fish she had ever eaten.

The following evening was the beginning of Charley's hand to hand combat training. They went down to the river and tossed out their hooks with a bobber. Charley planted the handle of each rod, and put a bell on the tip. If they hooked a fish, the bell would ring to alert them.

Kat picked up a stick and handed it to Charley. She pointed to a willow bush, saying, "That's a man coming at you with his fists. Protect yourself."

Charley swung the stick back and forth before it slipped out of his hand. Kat yelled, "You lost, Charley! You're beaten, and you might be dead."

She showed him how to handle the club, and threatened to beat him herself if he ever dropped it again. She made him repeat over and over. They trained until dark, when they pulled their fishing lines and headed home.

Kat made Charley practice the same moves for the next few evenings. As Charley improved, Kat made him face two willow bushes and then three. When he got better, Kat would hang things in the branches to resemble guns and knives. Charley would have to disarm the bushes under Kat's strict supervision.

Kat would yell, "Get the guns, then the knives, and only then go after your attackers. Be sure you know where they are at all times."

One day, Charley showed Kat how to tie the branches back with a slip knot. One of them would go into the bush and the other would release the slip knots one at a time. The fighter would battle, stopping the attackers with guns and knives as they popped out.

They practiced time after time until they got it perfect. Then they would re-arrange the weapons and start again. Occasionally a fish would bite and distract them completely. They had long discussions as they walked back and forth to the fishing hole.

Charley and Kat both loved nature, so that was most often their topic of conversation. Charley would stop each time they saw a track, to explain what animal had made it. He showed Kat many of the herbs and plants that were used for native medicine. She told him in turn about life on the ranch and how to heal the sick animals. They talked about family and friends. They were both loners who loved the wilderness.

Kat's body continued to heal. The wounds would leave scars, but there was nothing anybody could do to prevent it. She was having fun training Charley, which made her stronger every day. As soon as the scars on her back healed enough that she could ride in a car, she would have to leave, even though she hated to. Kat was happy in Angela's home.

Kat saw Dr. Singh one day for her check up. He looked carefully at all of her injuries. The bruises had almost faded away and the deep scratches were healing nicely.

"You heal very quickly," the doctor said. "I think you can safely do anything you did before."

Kat was happy that she was almost healed, but sorry that she had to leave. "Thank you," said Kat. "I guess I'll be leaving soon then." She left his office, thinking about planning her trip.

When supper was finished, Kat announced, "I'll be leaving in a few days. The doctor said I can travel now, so I better go back, check on my folks and stuff."

"You're welcome to stay as long as you want, Kat," Angela said.

"Yeah, you don't have to go," added Charley.

"No, I need to go back, for a while anyway, but I'll be back. That's a promise," Kat said sadly. "This is a wonderful place."

Iris and Wanda just sat quietly, knowing that her decision had been made. They would miss her, though.

"I sure don't feel like driving up the hill, though," said Kat.

"I heard it snowed on the hill yesterday," Wanda said.

"I'll see if anybody has been out and how the hill is tomorrow at work," Angela added. "They usually stop when they get back to town."

Kat excused herself and went to bed early. She was asleep when her head hit the pillow.

"I wonder who Richard really is," Wanda said.

"He sure didn't look like any of the other fishermen that come here," Iris added.

"Yes, it is kind of funny he came here all by himself. He sure isn't a fisherman," said Charley. "He didn't have any gear when he got here. He had to buy everything new. He didn't even have a rod or reel."

"He seemed to have lots of money though," added Angela. "He sure looked after Kat, and was really worried when she was missing."

"We'll probably never know who he really is," said Iris. "I wonder if Kat knows. He sure looked after her, and maybe he's just a good person."

They tossed around many different ideas of who Richard might be, but none of them knew for sure.

Kat was up very early the next morning. Iris had already been up for a while with coffee brewing, while she mixed the biscuit dough.

Charley dragged himself to the table with a social studies textbook. He often did his homework in the mornings. Evenings were free to fish and do boy stuff. Kat helped him with his homework as Iris watched and listened intently. Kat did not notice when she slipped away.

Iris returned a few minutes later. In her hands she carried a beautifully beaded buckskin bag. She held the bag out to Kat and said, "Kat, I'd like you to have this."

Kat took the bag and admired the beadwork. The object inside was quite heavy so Kat laid it on her lap and opened it. Kat was astonished to see an old dagger. It had a bone handle with bone inlay. When she pulled the blade from the scabbard, it gleamed like the morning sun.

"Thank you," Kat said, not really knowing what to say.

Iris said quietly, "You know where it came from, Kat. Always remember how it came to our village and the girl who wore it."

"Charley, would you keep it for me until I get a place of my own? Keep it safe and never sell it, no matter how much you're offered."

"Sure," answered Charley. He knew the legend of the warrior girl who had acquired it and saved the girls of the village. He also knew why Iris had given it to Kat, and was proud of her. She was the best friend Charley had ever had.

"I think maybe it's Spanish," said Iris, "but I don't know for sure." She poured coffee and got the biscuits from the oven. They quietly ate the biscuits with home-made jam.

Kat checked her car as well as she could, before she started it. It had not run for over a month, but fired right up and sat there idling. She spent the rest of the morning cleaning and polishing. It looked much better, when she was finished, she thought. If only it could climb the hill tomorrow.

Charley came home early that day. After a quick lunch he said, "Let's go fishing, Kat. Not much happening at school this afternoon." They grabbed their fishing gear and were off, to Charley's favorite fishing hole.

They chatted about things that interested them both, mostly to do with nature. Kat had some ideas of how they could start a business in Bella Coola that would help preserve the ecology of the valley while creating awareness of how important this unspoiled rain forest really is.

Charley laughed and said, "Kat, that's called 'ecotourism.' I've been reading about people who have started businesses like that. Some of them go broke, but some of them do quite well."

They decided that Charley should do more research, and if it looked feasible they would start a business when he finished school. He could be the river guide and take the people down in a drift boat.

Charley loved the idea. He would have to make a living, but did not want to leave the valley when he grew up. He began planning what he would need for equipment. They were busy designing the lodge when Kat got a bite. She brought the fish to shore so Charley could grab it. He quickly cleaned it and they headed home for supper.

Iris baked the fresh fish with her usual skill. Kat would miss Iris' cooking and the evenings at the table with everyone talking about their day; the legends that Iris would tell and Charley's adventures.

When supper was finished, Angela said, "Kat, I talked to a fellow who needs a ride to Williams Lake tomorrow. I told him you were driving out and could use the company. He has trucks and has to pick one up at Williams Lake. He runs the hill all of the time and will drive if you want. Marty's a good guy; you'll enjoy his company. He'll be here in the morning."

"That's great," said Kat. "I sure could use the company, and I think he can drive up the hill too. That's a job for a pro."

Iris knew Marty through a mutual friend, and said, "Yes, he's a nice fellow, sure treats the old people well. I think he lives in Firvale."

Iris had her usual coffee and biscuits ready when Kat got up. She ate her breakfast while everyone else gradually got up. Marty arrived, and, as they walked out to leave, everyone followed them. Kat gave each of them a big hug and promised to return soon. She noticed tears running down Wanda's cheeks. They had become good friends, even though Wanda did not talk much.

They crawled into the little car and were off. Kat drove slowly out of town onto the highway. Kokanee ran around a corner and followed her car, until something distracted him and he took off down an alley.

As they drove past Thorsen Creek, Kat asked, "Have you ever been to the petroglyphs, Marty?"

"Yes, I go there all the time. I'd sure like to know who made them and what they represent," he replied.

They talked about the petroglyphs for a minute before Marty began to describe their surroundings. He had been up and down the road hundreds of times, and knew every inch. He pointed out things on the mountains that Kat had not seen on her way in. He told her what lay up each valley they went by. He knew every house and most of the people who lived in them.

Kat thought Marty must have been raised in the valley, but he said, "No"; he had come from over the mountains in Alberta.

When they got to the bottom of the hill, they saw it was covered with fresh snow. Marty asked Kat to pull over behind a truck parked on the side of the road. The driver was out putting chains on the tires, so Marty went over to talk to him. He chatted for a minute with the driver before walking back.

Kat rolled down the window and Marty asked, "Do you have chains, Kat?"

"No," she answered.

"Your tires are getting a bit too smooth, so I think Ed should pull you up the hill, if that's okay."

"Sure," said Kat. "Would you drive my car up, please?"

The men hooked up a long rope while Kat switched seats. Marty hopped into the driver's seat, and they began their long, slow climb behind the truck, the chains ringing like bells down the valley below. Kat kept her window rolled down, even though it was cold. She was not sure why, but she found it impossible not to look over the cliff beside them, into the valley straight below.

They slowly went around switchback after switchback. The truck honked and stopped and the backup lights came on at a narrow ledge. Marty slipped the car into reverse, so they backed slowly down the hill to a switchback with the truck holding them on the taut rope, keeping them from sliding back over the cliff.

They stopped at the switchback where the road was wider, while a four wheel drive with chains slipped and slid slowly down the hill. When he was by, they resumed their slow ascent until they finally reached the top.

Kat got out and helped them unhook. She thanked Ed for the pull as she looked longingly at the wilderness valley below.

"You're the girl that was mauled by the bear, aren't you?" Ed asked.

"Yes," Kat answered.

"That must have been quite an experience. I'd sure like to hear about it sometime. If you ever have time when you're driving by, stop in for coffee. I live at Nimpa Lake. Ask anybody for directions to my place. I know them all."

"I'll do that," Kat replied. "I'll be back soon."

Kat and Marty let the truck go first, before leaving. It was colder at the top of the hill, and the wind was blowing. Snow covered the ground with a fresh sparkling white blanket. Kat was amazed at how much the climate could change in a few miles.

"I'd like to stop at Anaheim Lake for a few minutes, Marty," Kat said. "I have to drop off a 'Thank You' card at the store for some people I stayed with on the way out here."

"Good idea," Marty said. "I'd like to stretch and pick up some lunch. We've got a long drive ahead."

"Don't buy lunch," said Kat. "Iris packed us enough for a small army."

It was snowing when they drove into Anaheim Lake. The little town was quiet, with snow beginning to cover the cars parked on the street. Smoke came from every chimney in town. Kat could not see when she walked into the store from the bright snow outside.

"Well, look at that, it's Kat!" said a familiar voice. As her eyes adjusted, she saw Percy and Mae standing in front of her.

"My heavens, what happened to you, dear?" she said, looking at the scars on Kat's face.

"Grizzly," said Kat, elaborating only slightly on her experience. They talked for a few minutes until Kat gave them the "Thank You" card and said they had to carry on.

"Just a minute," Mae said, digging around in her old leather purse and pulling out an envelope. "I won this at the Williams Lake Stampede. It's for a trip to Las Vegas, and I won't use it. The flight is in a couple of days. I'd just have let it expire, so you might as well use it."

"Thanks," said Kat. "That sounds like fun. I could wait an extra week to find a job." She gave them both a long hug and walked through the fresh snow to the car where Marty waited.

The snow was beginning to blow across the highway, making the visibility quite poor. Kat drove carefully, watching for animals and vehicles on the road ahead. Marty broke the long silence suddenly by asking, "Do you believe in God, Kat?"

She looked over to where he sat, very serious, and answered, "Yes, I do, Marty."

"But you had a dream of talking animals and saw people from ancient times. How can you believe in God and believe in pagan religion?" Marty asked.

Kat replied, "Well, Marty, that's a question that I've been asking myself. The conclusion I've made is that God speaks to you in a language you can understand. Kind of the way we're communicating now. If you spoke to me in German, I wouldn't understand a word you said. The Arab world, at the time the scriptures were written, was a whole lot different than an Indian village on the Northern Pacific coast. Do you think anybody here had seen a desert or a camel or a donkey? These people lived in harmony with nature and depended on the animals for their survival."

"That's interesting, Kat," Marty said. "I've studied a lot of theology and the more I learn, the more questions I have. Would you mind describing the dream that you had, in detail? I'd sure like to hear it."

Every detail of the dream she had on the mountain that lonely night was still vivid in Kat's mind. She started at the very beginning and talked for miles until she was finished.

"Quite a story," said Marty when she was finished. "Do you think it was a message or just your mind playing tricks because you had been hurt so bad?"

"Good question," replied Kat. "I could argue either way. I was badly hurt, as well as being tired and alone, but I have never had a dream like that or been able to remember anything so vividly. It's like it happened an hour ago. The elders virtually described one of the girls who was dancing. They had no doubt in their minds that I had visited the other side. I've read about people who have had near-death experiences, but this was different than any of those. Have you ever experienced anything like that, Marty?"

"As a matter of fact, I have," answered Marty. "Would you like to hear about it?"

"I'd love to," Kat replied, as she drove along the seemingly endless highway.

"I'm not sure where to start, Kat. It was many years ago and it completely turned my life around," said Marty.

"I was a young punk criminal, didn't care about anything or anybody other than myself. I was addicted to booze, drugs, cigarettes and anything else that would give me a high. I'd do anything when I was stoned, from fighting to stealing or just going along with some criminal as long as there was something in it for me – booze, money or whatever. When the cops would try to take me in, I was usually stoned and would fight them. Once it took 8 cops to get me subdued. That was in the days before pepper spray, luckily for me. I'd be in and out of jail all the time. The only thing I didn't like about jail was the shortage of booze and drugs.

"I was a tough guy in jail, so life in there was easy. Nobody could ever beat me in a fight. Eventually, my crimes became more serious, and I found myself spending most of my time in prison. I became very depressed and began contemplating suicide.

"One night, I was lying on the floor of my jail cell, thinking of how I could end my life, when Jesus came to me. He stood in front of me and we talked for a long time. He told me how I was wasting away the life that God had chosen for me. He told me how important every day we have on this earth is, so we'd better not waste a minute. He talked about the great rewards that we receive by helping others, and being fair in everything that we do. He told me about the shallow happiness that we get from drug and alcohol addictions, and how they eventually destroy the body that God created just for you. Before He left, Jesus told me that I could be healed if I wanted to be, and would only be satisfied if I learned to live under God's rules.

"My life changed that night. I studied the Bible in jail and, when I got out, I went to Bible School as soon as I could. I studied to become a priest so I could spread the word of God and share my happiness with others.

"Kat, you can not believe how much happier I became in going from my world of addictions and crime into the world of God. I still laugh when I recall working on a pipeline crew one summer. I'd wake those poor guys up in the middle of the night to preach to them and introduce them to my preacher friends.

"I've mellowed a bit since then, so I don't preach to everyone I meet. I truly think that had Jesus not come to me that night, I would have been found dead in an alley somewhere from an overdose, or become so deranged as to take my own life. I'm now the satisfied, humble person that Jesus promised me that I could become if only I would try. I've never had any cravings either. When most people try to break addictions, they crave for years, but I haven't had any.

"Now a question for you, Kat. Was it just a dream, or did Jesus really contact me?"

Kat was quiet for a moment. "I guess we'll never know that answer for sure, but if it makes you a better person, you must believe it is real. Do we always need to prove everything? Maybe there are some things that we will never know for sure. I think everybody knows when they are doing wrong, but for some reason they still do it."

"Yes," Marty said. "I've studied religion for many years now and don't have the answer. Wars have been fought over religion, and in medieval times people were tortured. These are against the scriptures, but people have twisted the interpretations into whatever they want them to be."

Marty and Kat discussed the meanings of their dreams for hours as they rolled down the highway. Marty asked Kat question after question, trying to memorize every detail of her dream so he could research it when time permitted.

Kat dropped him off at a shop in Williams Lake where his truck was parked and ready to make the long trip back to the coast.

Kat wanted to make it over the Rockies the following day, so she pressed on. Snow swirled across the pavement, changing her vision constantly, and sometimes almost creating illusions. It was a bit better in the dark because of the contrast that the headlights created.

By the time she reached Kamloops, Kat was extremely tired. She decided to pull into a truck stop for coffee. The place was full of truckers who had stopped because of the weather. Their heads turned as Kat walked in and sat alone.

"How's the road?" said one of the fellows sitting close to her.

"It's not icy yet, but you can hardly see through the snow," Kat replied.

Truckers are an unusual bunch. They spend most of their lives alone in a truck, so they crave conversation when they get together. They are like a band of brothers who help each other whenever they can.

The conversation lasted for a long while, with Kat learning everyone's name and looking at pictures of their families. They told her amazing stories of places they had traveled in their huge machines, and about the fun they had when they were home with their families. Kat could tell that they loved what they did, even though they had to fight the loneliness at times. They had all missed birthdays, anniversaries, weddings and funerals, but accepted the fact that it was part of their job. The good times had to outweigh the bad.

When the truckers found out that Kat planned to sleep in her car, they were very concerned. It was cold out, so she could not run the engine for fear of carbon monoxide poisoning. They decided Kat should sleep in Greg's truck.

Greg had a big double bunk sleeper that he kept neat as a pin. He had shown her pictures of his wife and daughters. Kat could not stand the idea of sleeping in her car and wanted to save what money she had left for her trip to Las Vegas, so she accepted Greg's offer and they left for the night.

THE MUSHROOM PICKER

The trucks were angled side by side. All lit up, they filled the parking lot. Kat unrolled her bedroll in the top bunk and listed to the purr of the engine as she chatted with Greg. Within minutes, she was sleeping like a baby, safe and warm in spite of the blizzard that raged outside.

When Kat awoke, the engine in the truck was still purring quietly. Greg was quietly polishing the gauges in the dash. He looked over at the bunk where Kat was watching from and said, "Good morning, Kat. Looks like the storm's let up. You hungry? We might as well have breakfast. Then I've got to make a mile."

Kat hopped down out of her bunk and said, "Sure. Just let me comb my hair and straighten up a bit. I'm sure I look pretty rough this morning."

Kat did look rough, but Greg did not care. That was not the way he judged people.

"Don't worry," he said with a laugh. "I live in a house with four females. I know what mornings with girls are all about. My girls get all upset and don't want to go to school if they see a new pimple. My wife has to get the little one off to the sitter so she can go to work, and you should see that sometimes. My old buddy Mike says two men can spend the whole winter in an eight by eight cabin, but there isn't a section of land big enough for two women. Why is that, Kat?"

Kat thought as she combed her red hair, and finally said, "It must be because women are judged more on their looks than men. I think women are far more critical of themselves than men ever are."

They talked as they walked through the fresh snow toward the restaurant.

The truckers were all gathered in an intense conversation when they walked into the restaurant. They all looked in unison at Kat and Greg as they walked in.

"Sleep well?" said one of the old boys, grinning.

"Sure," Kat replied. "I see why you guys don't stay in motels. I slept better than I think I ever have. Greg kept hogging the covers, though," she said with a laugh.

They teased each other back and forth until another one of the truckers came in and sat down beside Greg.

"Hi, Jake," Greg said. "Which way you headin'? Just wonder how the road is."

"Just coming from the coast," he replied. "It wasn't too bad from the coast, but I hear the mountain passes are really a mess this morning. I've been talking to some drivers who were holed up in the pass overnight."

Kat's heart sank. She had to cross the Rockies today, and did not want to have to spend the night in her car. She would freeze to death.

"Sorry to be so rude, but I forgot to introduce you," said Greg. "Jake, Kathy Townsend, known as Kat. Kat, this is Jake."

"Kathy Townsend," said Jake. "Kind of got a ring to it. Mind if I call you Kathy Townsend instead of Kat? I think it sounds better."

"Sure," said Kat.

The only time she had ever been called by her full name before was when she had managed to get herself into trouble, and Gram would hunt her down and scold her. "Kathy Townsend, what will you ever amount to if you keep acting this way? Mercy. I just don't know what to do with you sometimes," she would say, and then stomp away. Kat missed Gram.

Greg brought her out of her trance when he said, "Kat's got to go over the pass today, Jake. Would you keep an eye on her if she follows you?"

Jake thought for a long minute before asking, "What are you driving, Kathy Townsend?"

She laughed to herself before answering, because Jake sounded so funny. "My car. It's a little Firefly."

"A Firefly?" Jake repeated. "Would you mind if I put your Firefly in my trailer and hauled you and your Firefly across the mountains, Kathy Townsend? I'm running back empty and I could use the weight."

"That would be absolutely wonderful!" Kat exclaimed. "Are you sure it's not an inconvenience?" These truckers are the most generous people I've ever met, and polite too, Kat thought, as she graciously accepted Jake's offer.

"No problem at all," answered Jake. "Greg and I will run it over and load while you have a coffee with this bunch of misfits. Watch yourself and don't let these old dogs talk you into anything," he laughed as he and Greg walked out.

"Fine pair of boys, those two," said one of the old truckers at the next table. "You'll be one lucky lady if you snag a man like that, young lady."

"You guys all seem nice," replied Kat. "I've heard stories about how nasty truck drivers are, but you guys have sure been good to me."

"Yeah," said one of the other drivers. "A lot of people think we are the scum of the earth, but we stick together and help people who appreciate it. Most people just snub us. We always know what's happening up and down the road. Talk to each other up and down the highway. After a few years of this, you know everybody who drives a rig."

"That Jake's some driver," said another old driver. "He's been on every road in North America and hauled everything from apples to alligators."

They visited and laughed until Greg and Jake returned, never once asking about the huge scars across Kat's face.

"The Firefly's on board, Kathy Townsend," said Jake. "Shall we be off across the mountains?"

"Let's do it," replied Kat. "I truly enjoyed meeting you fellows, and when I get the lodge built in Bella Coola, you are all invited. I'll take you all fishing myself."

They all said farewell as Jake and Kat left for the truck.

Jake's truck was also neat and clean. He took off his shoes and put on clean slippers when he got in. Kat kicked her shoes off so she would not get the floor wet and dirty. Jake released the parking brakes and they were off. Kat had not seen her little car, but assumed it was tucked away in the trailer behind them.

"Have you been to Bella Coola, Kathy Townsend?" Jake asked. "I've always wanted to fish the river there but I've never made it."

"Yes, that's where I'm coming from. I've been there for the past couple of months. Went there to pick mushrooms and ended up getting mauled by a huge grizzly bear. I've been staying with a native family."

"Wow!" Jake said. "Is that how you got those scars?"

"Yeah," Kat replied. "The elders said the bear just marked me. If he'd wanted to kill me, he sure could have. He was huge."

"Did you fish there?" asked Jake.

"Charley taught me how to fish the river," replied Kat. "I've fished every day for a month."

"How do you know where the fish are?" Jake asked.

"Just imagine the river with no water in it," replied Kat. "The salmon travel in the channels and rest in the pools. A lot of people just toss their hook into the shallow water and hope to catch a fish, but the chances of getting anything there are slim. You have to feel the river through your line."

"Can you catch them on flies?" asked Jake. "I live for fly fishing. Best sport known to mankind."

"Sure," said Kat. "Just read the water."

Suddenly Jake ground the truck to a halt at a pullout. He crawled into the sleeper, and came back holding a small box. When he opened it, Kat saw it was filled with fishing flies.

"Tied these flies myself," said Jake as he took them out one by one and showed them to her. Each one was a work of art, gleaming with brilliant hues or the dull color of animal hair, cleverly shaped to resemble an insect or larva. "Do you think any of these would work for salmon?"

Kat picked a few that looked like they may work, saying, "I think these would catch fish, but I'd have to ask Charley for sure."

"One day I'll go to Bella Coola and try them," said Jake. "Did any of the natives ever tell you any of their legends? I've heard that they have legends that have been passed down through generations but have never actually been told one."

"Sure," Kat answered. "Iris used to tell us legends every evening after supper. I don't know if I can remember them completely. I've only heard them a few times, and they have so many."

"Would you tell me one?" asked Jake.

"I'll try to remember," Kat answered. "But you'll have to bear with me.

"The Nuxalk have very ancient beliefs of how their world is and was. There is a world above and a world below our level. Man came down to earth a long time ago, and could change between human and animal forms at will. Okay, here goes.

"A long time ago there was a man who lost everything in a gambling game. His wives, his house, his hunting gear and all of his things were lost. His father was ashamed and disgusted with his son's selfish deeds, so he told the people of the village to move away and leave his son to starve.

"The villagers packed up everything and moved away. Only an old slave woman felt sorry for him and hid some embers in a shell. When they all left, he went to the place she had told him about and blew the embers into a fire, which he kept going. He could find no food though, and wasted away to a skeleton. He lay down to die and covered himself with moss.

"As he lay there, he heard a woman's wail. He thought to himself, 'That can be no human. If she comes I will die, which I will do anyway. It does not matter.'

"The voice kept calling from closer and closer. Suddenly, a woman appeared with long braids and two blankets. 'My father has sent me to help you,' she said. 'He has seen your suffering.'

"He did not know it, but the woman was Wolf. She massaged the man with mountain goat grease until he felt better. He found that he was gaining more supernatural strength each time she massaged him, so pretended to be weak until he was satisfied.

"The woman asked him to go home with her, but the snow was deep, so they had to double on her snowshoes.

"When they got to her house, there was an old man there who was her father. He asked the man to marry his daughter, which he was happy to do. The man taught the old man the gambling game, which the old man came to love, so he gave the man the power to always win at it.

"They lived in Wolf's house and the man was happy. She had a son, who grew very fast. When the child was about two, the man grew tired of living in Wolf's house and wanted to go back to his old home.

"They were willing, but Old Wolf told the man that he must never let smoke drift over his wife. The man could not understand, so he asked Old Wolf to explain. Old Wolf said that if he paid attention to any other woman, it would be as though his wife was sitting in smoke, and he could not see her. She would know if she was sitting in smoke.

"The man returned to his old home with his wife and son, and began to gamble again. With the power Wolf had given him, he often won and accumulated a wealth of food and slaves. The man was careful not to look at any other woman for fear of Wolf's threat.

"One day he was at the river getting water, when one of his ex-wives came down with her dog. The dog ran up to him and he petted the dog and played with it. When he got back, his wife dropped a piece of mountain goat sinew into the pail that had the power to tell if he had shown affection to another. If he had, it would curl up into a tight coil, which it did. She asked, 'Why did you let smoke drift over me?' and left for her father's house.

"The man was heartbroken, and determined to follow his wife and child. Their tracks led under the lakes, but he pursued until he neared Wolf's village. At the lower end of the lake was a hut where the old man lived. 'Have you seen my wife, daughter of Wolf?' he asked. 'Yes, she came several days ago. She is afraid of you, so she doesn't come outside, but the boy does. Wait here and you will see him.' The boy came soon after, and when he got near, the father grabbed him. He told the boy, 'Tonight, you must cry and say you must go outside. Others will try to take you out but you must insist that your mother take you.'

"That night, the boy cried. The old woman and girls tried to take him, but he would not stop crying until the mother finally took him outside. She was afraid that her husband might be stalking her.

"As soon as the wife was clear of the house her husband grabbed her and embraced her. This proved his love for her, so she was not angry any more.

"She insisted that they return to her house. He remained at the Wolf village and eventually became a wolf himself. The man never returned to the land of the mortals.

"That's it. How was it?"

"That was great. Do you know any more, Kathy Townsend?"

"I'm not much of a storyteller and I don't know how good I'll do, but I'll try," Kat said.

"This one is about the boy who visited the home of the fish.

"Once, a long, long time ago, there was a boy who was very poor. All he owned was a goat skin blanket. He was very hungry and he had no friends.

"One day he decided to commit suicide. The ice was breaking up in Bella Coola River, so he had to jump from sheet to sheet. He would jump onto a block of ice, run across and jump to another. The boys from the village followed and yelled at him to stop. When he reached a large opening at the middle of the river, he jumped into the freezing water.

"The boy did not drown. He found a road under the water that led him to the land of the herring. He kept following the path until he came to the land of each species of fish; oolachan, sockeye salmon, humpback salmon, steel head and finally to the land of the Coho. Each species of fish lived in its own country, with the Coho being the farthest, so they were last to come up it.

"He had been in the fish countries for only a short time when the great salmon boat headed for Bella Coola River, and the boy returned home on it. He became wealthy and famous because of his adventure.

"That's it," said Kat, "If you want to hear more legends, I'll introduce you to Iris. She knows them all."

"I'd like to take you up on that, Kathy Townsend. If I ever have time, I'm going out there. I could listen to those legends for hours. I sure hope someone has enough sense to record them all."

"I have a daughter about your age," Jake said, "It's a tough time, isn't it? Some days you want to be all grown up and sometimes just a kid. I think it's harder for girls these days."

"Yes," Kat replied. "It seems that I never thought much about birth or death or God and religion or what I really wanted to do with my life. When I spent the night on the mountain and had that strange dream, I figured a few things out, though."

"Would you mind telling me about your experiences, Kathy Townsend?"

"Sure," Kat said as she began telling her story. She described her lonely and painful adventure in detail, while Jake listened quietly.

When she was finished, Jake said, "That's quite a story. You're lucky to be alive. Can I see the nugget you found in your pocket?"

Angel had had the nugget mounted and attached to a leather thong, which hung around Kat's neck. She removed it and showed it to Jake. He looked at it as he drove around the bends.

"Isn't it something?" he said. "I think we should stop for lunch. We've got some tough sledding ahead."

The service stations in the pass were few and far between, so they pulled in at the next stop. The mountains glistened with fresh snow and the wind howled outside.

Kat had not noticed how bad the road really was while she had chatted with Jake. It shocked her when she stepped out of the truck. They bought coffee and snacks and raced back to the comfort of the waiting truck.

Jake wheeled back onto the highway like an old pro. When he had finished gearing up, Kat said, "Your turn to tell me your legend, Jake."

Jake pondered for a while and then laughed and said, "Sure, but it's not ancient."

"That's okay," said Kat. "I don't think there's an age limit."

"It's called, 'Boy and the Pumphouse Door'. Once upon a time there was a boy named Jake. Jake had two sisters who loved to play tricks on him. Jake thought his mother was a tyrant, because she gave her children a good lickin' when they were bad, which they often were. The family lived on a farm in the north.

"One winter it was extremely cold, and on this particular day it was forty below zero when the children were sent out to do chores. The girls had been cooped up in the house for a few days, and hadn't been able to pull any pranks on poor Jake for fear of punishment from their mother. Their minds worked quickly in the cold, so it was easy for them to devise a prank. 'Jake, come over here,' said the older sister.

"He walked over, suspicious that something was up. 'I dare you to put your tongue on the door handle.' It was a large steel handle and Jake knew it would sting. Jake was a very wise boy so he refused, but the sisters taunted him unmercifully. 'Sissy, coward, wimp,' they called him, and said, 'I'll tell Mom you were smoking.'

"Jake got angry, and walked over and put his tongue directly on the steel door handle. It instantly froze and stuck there. Jake couldn't pull it away and stood there screaming. Finally his mother came out with a tea kettle full of warm water and poured it over his tongue until it came loose. She scolded him for being so stupid and hunted down the sisters, who were hiding. They all got a good lickin'. End of legend."

Kat clapped and laughed, "Good legend, Jake. I wonder who the boy was," and laughed again.

They were into the high Rockies when it began to snow. Visibility was getting poor, so the traffic was moving slower. A loud blue truck, heavy with a load of lumber, roared by them on a downhill stretch. Jake was on his tail by the time they crested the next hill.

"Must be a new driver," Jake said seriously. "He sure doesn't know how to run in the mountains. Sure hope he makes it. That's a lot of weight on his trailer, hard to stop with that load."

They followed the truck for mile after mile. He would race down the hills with no regard for curves or other motorists. Then he would crawl back up the other side.

Jake was patient and stayed behind. "You get too tired if you let other drivers bother you," Jake told Kat. "At the end of the day, you'll make more miles if you just keep your cool and don't get impatient."

They passed slowly through the alpine town of Golden. Jake followed the lumber truck slowly up the long climb out of town, but when they started down hill, the truck was soon lost from their sight.

The curves became tighter as they made their descent down the mountain. As they rounded a tight bend, they saw to their dismay that the lumber truck had slid into a bridge, high above a stream. The trailer still sat on the road, but the truck had gone through and hung, suspended high above the river, held only by the weight of the trailer.

"Hang on," Jake yelled as he swerved around the trailer and ground to a halt. They both watched in horror, as the driver, dazed from the impact, stepped out of the cab, only to plunge to the river below

Kat jumped from the truck before it had even stopped. She climbed over the snow bank on the side of the road and hurried, slipping and sliding, over the snow. She could see the driver flailing in the water as he was slowly being swept downstream.

Kat ran to the edge of the ice that protruded part way into the stream and dived in. The water was not very deep, but was freezing cold. Kat knew that she could not last very long, so she would have to be fast.

She half swam, half waded along the river, until she could grab the man by his collar. He was quiet now. She pulled and dragged with all of her might to get him to the bank, where a group of truck drivers were preparing to haul him up to the highway.

When she got close to the ice, she felt strong hands lift her from the frigid water. She watched as the men carefully laid the driver onto a makeshift stretcher. The men rolled up their coats and placed them on each side of his head and down his body to immobilize him, before they bound him tightly onto a stretcher with duct tape. Somebody put a blanket around Kat and she felt herself being carried up the hill. She could see that the man on the stretcher was alive and conscious once again.

A woman in a motor home held the door open to let the men carry Kat inside. She chased them back out, and quickly stripped off Kat's wet clothes. She dried Kat from head to toe, before dressing her in some warm clothes of her own, and putting a warm blanket around her.

"Keep this stuff," she said. "It's just some clothes I keep in here for camping."

Kat just sat and shivered as she drank the hot coffee that the lady had given her. When she began to warm up, she thanked the lady and went out to find Jake. The ambulance was just leaving, with its lights flashing and its siren wailing.

Kat found Jake talking with some of the other drivers who had helped with the rescue. She said she was ready to leave, so they made their way back to the truck and quietly slipped away.

"I wonder who that girl was?" said the woman in the motor home to her husband, as they drove along the highway once again. "Did you see the scars on her face?"

"Yes," said the retired pilot. "She must have been in a car accident or something."

"They were nothing, compared to the scars on her back," the woman said. "They were all across her back from top to bottom. What do you think could have done that?"

"I really don't know," he answered. "She sure is a brave little thing, jumping into the river like that. By rights, she should have drowned in that freezing water and all."

They talked about Kat for hours. She was the unknown girl who would never be forgotten by any of the people who were there that day.

"You okay, Kathy Townsend?" Jake asked, as they rolled down the highway.

"Yeah, I'm fine," Kat replied, as she huddled in her blanket. "Just having a bit of trouble warming up."

"You were amazing back there," Jake said. "You were in the river before I got this rig stopped. I thought you were going to drown. Weren't you afraid?"

"No," replied Kat. "I haven't had any fear since I came off the mountain with Charley. Sometimes I have to think about how to remain safe and not do anything stupid, but I'm never afraid any more. Maybe some day I'll get that emotion back. Maybe it's what the Elders call becoming a warrior, and it's something that happens after a trauma. Truthfully, I don't know for sure."

"You saved that guy's life back there. He may never see you again, to thank you, but I'm sure he will if he gets the chance. His wife and kids, too. You know, that could have been any of us drivers. We all understand that and try to help each other."

"Those guys with the stretcher sure seemed to know their stuff. They worked like paramedics. Where did that guy ever get the idea of using duct tape to hold him on the stretcher?"

"I'm not sure," said Jake, "but it sure was a good idea. That guy might have a broken neck, and that may stop him from becoming paralysed. Drivers see a lot of accidents, and talk about them at the truck stops. The better ideas travel pretty fast in this business. By tomorrow, there will be truckers sitting around tables in Texas, talking about what you just did to save a man's life. You'll be famous, Kathy Townsend." They laughed as they drove along.

Kat must have fallen asleep, and it was foggy when she woke up. It was pitch dark, and Jake was busy backing up the rig. He stopped abruptly and hopped out. Kat soon watched her little car pull up beside the truck. Jake jumped back in and held his hands over the defrost duct to warm them.

"Your car's ready to roll, Kathy Townsend," he said. "Better let it warm up for a few minutes." He quizzed her as to where she was going, and didn't let up until he was convinced that she would be safe. He gave her his phone numbers and his daughter's.

"If you ever need help, just call until you get somebody, or go to a truck stop and talk to the long haulers. Mention my name and they'll give you a hand," Jake said. He escorted her to her car and gave Kat a hug. She was sure she could see a tear glistening on his cheek, in the headlights. She put her Firefly in gear and drove away.

The lights were still on at Smiley's when Kat drove up. The door was locked, but she could see the silhouette of Greta washing the floor. Kat banged on the door and waited. She heard the bolt slide and the door opened. Greta looked at her before rushing out and hugging her breath away, all the time howling like a banshee for Smiley.

Smiley thought Greta was being attacked or robbed or something, and came racing out with his old shotgun. When he saw it was Kat, he set the gun down and hugged them both. When they were all over their excitement, Smiley said, "Let's go inside. It's darned cold out here," and led the way into the restaurant.

Smiley poured hot coffee as they sat down at the large table.

"Vat happened to you face?" Greta asked Kat with great concern. Kat gave a very short account of the bear attack that had left the scars. She was very careful not to upset these dear old people, who cared so much for her.

"Are you all right now?" asked Smiley. "We were all very worried when nobody heard from you."

"I had the best care that I could have got anywhere in the world," Kat replied. "I stayed with a native family while I recovered. I didn't call because I didn't want to worry anyone. Have you heard from my dad?"

"Yes," said Smiley. "That woman left him for another man as soon as she had all of his money spent. He's back living at the Ranch. It's the best thing that could have happened, Kat. She was just using your dad and hoping one day he'd get a big inheritance. When she found out that you got the Ranch, she went nuts and wanted to file a claim against the estate. When he wouldn't, she packed up all those deadbeat kids of hers and moved in with someone else. Good riddance, I say."

Greta smiled and said, "Yah, me too."

"That's the best news I've had in a long time," said Kat. "She's a bad one, but my dad's an honorable man, so he wouldn't throw her out, once he'd married the old bag. I'd have sicked the dog on her."

They sipped their coffee. "What else is new around the area?" asked Kat.

"Well, not a lot," said Smiley. "I think Sprig needs to go on a diet, she's getting so fat. Oh, yeah, there's an Indian gal bought a ranch out by your dad. She doesn't have a clue about ranching and buys everything at the auction mart that she thinks needs a good home. Sometimes those Rosehill and Daines boys won't even take her bids if they know the animal's too sick. Pretty honest boys, that bunch. They try not to stick their customers with anything bad. That's why they're still in business and they've got a good reputation.

"Anyway, your dad helps her all he can, but you should see her place. There are dogs and chickens and donkeys and horses everywhere. Folks around here are waiting for her to go broke, so they can grab up her land cheap. I hope she hangs on, just to show those vultures. Her name's Nika. Nobody knows where she's from. Somebody said she was on a reservation in the States and managed to borrow some money from one of the banks up here.

"She must not have much, judging by the truck she drives. Your dad calls it, 'Old Brockle,' because it looks like an old brockle faced cow, with rust spots all over it. I think your dad and her have taken a bit of a shine to each other."

"Ever hear about my mom?" Kat asked.

"I think things are about the same with her, Kat," Smiley answered. "I never see her because she never comes in here, but I haven't heard any of the customers mention anything unusual about her."

"I'm going to run over and see Dad," Kat said. She was rested from her sleep in the truck, and wanted to see him. She said good-bye to Smiley and Greta, and left with a promise to return in the morning.

Everything was dark when Kat drove down the laneway into the Ranch. She got out and banged on the door. She tried it and it was unlocked, so she walked into the kitchen and hollered, "Anybody home?" before sitting down to the table.

Her dad called down from upstairs, "What's all the commotion down there? Don't you know it's two o'clock in the morning? A man needs his sleep, you know."

As he came down the old stairway, he saw her and yelled, "Kat, I've been worried sick about you. Where've you been?" as he ran over and gave her a bear hug. He held her at arm's length, looking closely at her.

"What on earth happened to you?" he asked. He sat down, watching her closely.

"It was a grizzly bear, Dad. Got me on the back too." She lifted the bulky sweatshirt that the lady had given her, and showed him the marks on her back, which he inspected in detail.

"You're lucky to be alive, Kat. Why didn't you call me?" he asked.

"Well, Dad, by the time I was found, I knew I'd be okay, so I decided not to call and worry anyone," Kat replied.

"Tell me the whole story, Kat. I'd sure like to hear it, and you really should have called me," her dad said.

Kat related the details of the trip over the mountains and the people she met. Then she told him about her mushroom picking fiasco. When she got to the part about the bear attack, she went into greater detail. She told him about her dream and how Charley had found her, and how his family had nursed her back to health. She finished off by telling him about her trip back and how she had fished the man from the river.

By the time Kat was finished, two hours had elapsed. Her dad just sat there in awe, amazed that his daughter had been through so much while he remained totally unaware. He had not spoken a word the entire time, but had listened intently to each and every detail.

When she had finished, he said, "Your grandfather would be very proud of you, Kat. You remind me so much of him. I wish he could have told you about some of his adventures, but he just couldn't. It seemed that excitement found him, much as it does you."

"I would have liked to hear them, Dad, but I understand," said Kat. "I guess that was always why he was after me to defend myself. I fought a lot of bushes with that old stick, while he criticized me. He would never let up and I thank him for it now. I'm sure he's the reason that I'm alive today. It would have been easy to give up, that night on the mountain."

"How about you, Dad?"

He told her how Sheila had flipped out when she found that Kat had inherited the land. She had spent what money her dad had inherited, in a couple of weeks, and then pulled out with another man.

Dad was happy that she was gone. His life with her had been horrible. She had found a legal loophole that proved their marriage had never been legal, so she had immediately married the other fellow. Dad was now a free man.

"Tell me about your new neighbor," Kat said, with a knowing grin.

Dad pleaded ignorance and just said, "You'll just have to meet her, Kat. She's not much of a farmer, but she's learning. I think you'll like her."

Kat crawled onto the sofa and fell instantly asleep.

The aroma of coffee and bacon filled the house, as Kat awoke. She wandered slowly out, and gave her dad an affectionate hug. She's changed since she's been gone, he thought. She must be growing up. They proceeded to enjoy the wonderful breakfast Dad had prepared.

As they were clearing the table, a rusty old pickup raced up the lane and a woman with a buckskin jacket and long black braids came to the door. Her dad opened the door and the woman came in. She was in a total frenzy.

"It's Buster," she said. "He must have found another porcupine and his nose is full of quills. Would you mind coming over and helping me pull them out?"

"Sure," Dad said. "Nika, this is my daughter, Kat. Kat, this is Nika."

"I've heard a lot about you, from your father, Kat. He's pretty proud of you."

They gathered up some gloves and pliers and all piled into the cab of "Old Brockle." Nika fired the truck up in a cloud of blue smoke, and jerked it around until they were on the laneway. "Sorry, I'm not used to driving a standard," she said.

The old truck had a bad miss in the engine, and was in dire need of a new muffler. It rattled every time they hit a bump. "The poor woman," thought Kat. "She does need some help." When they drove into her farmyard, they were met by a rag tag bunch of dogs of all shapes and sizes. The dogs licked them and played around them as they got out. They were the friendliest bunch of mutts that Kat had ever seen.

Dad put on a pair of heavy gloves and grabbed the little Spaniel with quills in his nose, as he ran by. He handed the dog to Kat and she gently laid him on his back and kneeled astride him, holding firmly onto his front legs. A well-dressed young woman came out of the house and asked if she could help. "Yes," said Nika, "go into the house and boil some water."

When she had gone, Nika said, "Sorry, Brenda is a city girl. She'd faint if she saw this. That's what they do in the Westerns when they want to get rid of somebody, isn't it?"

They all had a good laugh, as Dad removed the quills from Buster's nose. Buster was small, but it was all Kat could do at times to hold him. Dad had to cut the ends off the bigger quills and deflate them, before he could pull them out.

When they were finished, they all stepped back before Kat let go. She was sure Buster would attack her when she let him loose, so she let go and stood up in one motion. Buster got up and came over and licked Kat affectionately, then walked around and licked the others.

Brenda came out of the house carrying a teakettle of boiling water. She looked around slowly, knowing something was up.

"Tea time?" Dad asked with a chuckle. Brenda smiled and turned back, with the others following her into the house.

Kat noticed that it was sparsely furnished, but a brand new laptop computer sat on the old sofa.

"Kat, I'd like you to meet my good friend, Brenda. She's up to visit me from Denver. We went to university together." Kat could not figure out why someone with a university education would be ranching themselves broke on the edge of the Canadian Rockies, but she had met a lot of eccentric people lately.

They had tea at the old round table, while Nika talked about her animals. They all made a tour of her barnyard, so Nika could show them her menagerie.

A little donkey came strolling over, and Brenda slipped him a sugar cube. "This is 'Honkey'," she said. "He is my favorite."

The place was more like a petting zoo than a working ranch, Kat thought, and she'll go broke by spring if she doesn't change the operation. Kat was nonetheless impressed that somebody would actually give these friendly animals a home. She wished she could help.

"See you tonight," Nika said, as she dropped them off.

"What was that all about, Dad?" Kat asked.

"Oh, she wants us to come over for supper tonight," he answered.

"She's going to go broke if she doesn't change her ranching operation soon, Dad, She's losing money. She's losing money on every animal on the place. I like what she's doing, but she'll lose it all. And that old Brockle truck of hers! It's like those old sway back horses she's got. They've seen their better days. I've been trying to figure out what we can do to help her."

"Don't worry, Kat. I know you like her and are worried about her, but she'll be fine," Dad said.

Kat went over to Smiley's for a while, until it was time for the bar to open. She walked in and stood in the shadows for a minute watching her mother, to make sure she was sober. She walked up to the bar and said, "Hi, Mom, how are you?"

Her mother looked up and began to cry. "Oh my God," she said. "What happened to your face?" she wailed.

"A bear, Mom, but I'm okay now." They talked for a few minutes until Kat said she had to leave. Her mother was very fragile, and it was easy to upset her, so Kat kept their meeting very short.

D ad was dressed to the nines when he came down the stairs to go to Nika's. Kat thought he was slightly overdressed to go have supper with a poor native lady in a buckskin jacket, but he knew best. She had not seen him dressed in suit and tie in years. He still polishes up pretty good, she thought.

Nika had the table set with an old lace tablecloth and candles when they arrived. Nika and Brenda were both dressed like they were going to the opera. Nika's braids sparkled in the firelight from old stone fireplace. Brenda served them all drinks, but Kat just had a Coke.

Supper was Cornish game hen with an assortment of side dishes. Kat was more confused than ever when she looked around the room.

When they were finished supper and the table was cleared Nika looked at Kat and cleared her throat, saying, "Kat, I'm not who I seem. My name isn't really Nika, its Monika. I just shortened it. I'm not really an Indian, I'm from German descent. Would you like to hear my story, Kat?"

"Sure, I'd love to." Kat answered, surprised to hear something like that and wondering what she had to hide.

"I'm a geologist from Oklahoma, Kat. I used to live the American dream. I had new cars and expensive holidays. Everything I wanted, I would buy, and think nothing of it. I worked hard enough, though.

"One day I got very sick and ended up in the hospital. I met an old man there who had some untapped oil properties in Canada that he wanted to sell cheap. He didn't want them any more so I bought them. When I started checking the seismograph data that he gave me with the mineral properties, I saw the best structures that I had ever seen. I called Brenda and we checked them over and over.

"It was a lot of risk to drill our first oil well. We both mortgaged everything we owned, and I signed over half of the properties to her. The first well came in like gangbusters and we kept drilling. I had so much money that I couldn't spend it fast enough. I surrounded myself with "yes-men" and supported the lot of them. They used me, Kat. Eventually they would have either broke me or killed me for my money.

"Then I got sick again. The only one who came to visit me in the hospital was Brenda. When I got out of the hospital, I flew up to Calgary to have a look at our property. That's when I fell in love with this place. I bought the ranch and flew back to Oklahoma. The first thing that I did when I got back was to boot out all of the leeches who were living off of me. Then I sold all of the houses and fancy cars, even the Jag. I got rid of all of that stuff.

"Brenda and I decided that she would run the business so I could change my identity. I turned myself into a native woman and moved to the ranch. Brenda comes here whenever she gets too stressed. I started frequenting the local auction marts, and that's where I met your dad. He's a lot more real than all those shallow characters that I used to hang with put together, (and kind of cute too,)" she winked.

"Your dad told me today that you were worried about me going bankrupt, Kat. Please don't worry about my finances, I have more money in the bank than I could spend in a lifetime, and more coming in every day. I'm just living the life that I chose to live, and if people find out I have a lot of money, the leeches will be back, and I'll have to move again. Only your dad and Brenda know who I really am. Will you please keep my secret, Kat?"

"Sure, I'd be glad to," said Kat. "But Monika, you're not much of a rancher and a pretty watered down Indian. One day you may even have to consider turning the Brockle out to pasture. Boy, you had me going, the other day when you had the suspenders on your bib overalls mended with wire I was feeling pretty sorry for you. What were those yellow things that you had hooked onto your suspenders?"

Monika laughed like a fiend and replied. "When you live like I have, you don't learn to sew. When my strap broke on my overalls I was out in the barn and there was some wire hanging there so that's what I used. The only problem was that whenever I bent over, the wire would poke me, so I found some yellow electrical connectors in the garage and screwed them onto the ends of the wire. It worked perfectly."

Kat laughed and said. "You just might make a pretty good rancher after all. Even my Gramps would have been proud of you."

Kat looked over and saw that her dad and Brenda were both in stitches.

"I'm going to Las Vegas tomorrow," Kat said, after things had calmed down. "A friend of mine gave me a ticket that she'd won. Rooms and bus transfers are included. I'm too young to gamble, but I would like to see Las Vegas. I'm sure there must be something that I could do there. Then I need to get serious about finding a job and make some money."

"I go there all of the time for meetings," said Brenda. "Too bad I wasn't going there this week. I could show you around."

"I sure don't miss that place," Nika added. "I've lost a bundle there at times. I wouldn't trade my barnyard for the glitter of the Strip."

Dad said, "I've never been there, and could care less if I ever saw the place. Just not much of a gambler I guess. I've always had to work too hard for my money to gamble it away."

"What's the Strip like?" Kat asked.

"It's unlike any place you've ever been before," said Brenda, "The hotels are huge, and all of the newer ones have a theme. You'll have to see it to believe it."

"I'd like to go to Bella Coola and see those petroglyphs that Kat was telling me about, maybe do a little salmon fishing," Dad said. "I'm not much of a traveller, but I'd like to go there and see where Kat was attacked by the bear, and follow the trail back down. Sounds like an interesting place. I'd also like to thank the family who took care of her while she was laid up."

"Is that how you got those scars?" asked Brenda. "Would you mind telling me about the bear attack, or would it bother you?"

Kat replied, "Yes, a Grizzly gave me those scars, and there's more on my back." She told them about the adventure, as they stared at her in awe. They could hardly believe what they were hearing, but they knew that every word was true.

When she finished, they insisted on seeing the scars on her back. They felt sorry for Kat, having to wear those scars for the rest of her life, but were ladies who did not judge people only by their looks. They both knew that Kat was tough and would not be intimidated, but those scars would change the way people looked at her. Nika knew how the change of her name from Monika had changed her life. Now she understood better about racism and discrimination.

The hour was late when Kat and her dad headed back to their ranch. Honkey came out of the shadows as the ladies saw them off, and Brenda sneaked him another sugar cube as she said goodbye. Kat gunned the Firefly and they drove off through a gauntlet of stray dogs that followed them down the driveway.

"I've never thought about a person having too much money before," said Kat. "I can sure see where it could create problems, though. Nika's lucky that she made her break when she did."

"Yes, she sure is," said Dad. "I'd never really thought about it either until recently. I've been studying the lives of celebrities. They have the same problem, but most of them can't escape. They must always have people after their money, people who couldn't give a hoot about them."

"Looks like Brenda's got her hands full running their oil company," said Kat, as they drove along.

"Yes, but she's cool about it. I think she likes what she's doing for now, and she'll make a change when the time is right. Smart pair of gals, those two."

They were laughing as they tramped through the snow to the old farmhouse. Ice fog was just beginning to settle, causing the air to sparkle under the yard light. Kat was torn about whether to leave this beautiful place for Las Vegas, but she knew that she could not make a comparison to a place she had never seen. She had to go.

Dad got a couple of Cokes from the fridge and sat down at the kitchen table across from Kat. He handed her one and asked, "So, what do you think of Nika, Kat?"

"Well." Said Kat. "I really don't think it's me we're worried about, Dad. I think she's great. I like people who can think for themselves. I laugh at those money-grabbing developers around here who want to get her land though. It would serve them right if she bought all of the land that came up for sale around here. But Dad, she really did have me worried that she'd go broke. She's really not much of a rancher. What about you, Dad? You got a crush on her?"

"We're just good friends, Kat," he said, making his way up the stairs. "Time to hit the hay," he said, as he disappeared around the landing.

Kat and Dad were just finishing breakfast when the Brockle came bouncing up the lane. Nika and Brenda jumped out with armloads of suitcases and bags. Dad held the door as they walked in and dumped the stuff in a pile on the kitchen floor.

"We decided that you needed a bit of help to get ready for your trip, Kat," said Brenda. "Better to look a bit classy when you go to Vegas."

The girls had picked out some expensive luggage for her, so that she would not look out of place.

"Up on the chair," said Nika. "We're going to give you a makeover."

Kat had always been just a country girl. She had never thought of wearing makeup or about hairstyles. She had always been more concerned with the horses and cattle. This was all new to her, but she was in the hands of experts, she thought.

Dad had had enough. He put on his coveralls and winter boots to go do the chores. He stayed out until his fingers were about frozen. When he came back in, the women had the kitchen transformed into a beauty salon and were so busy they did not even know he was there. He got into his truck and drove to Smiley's for coffee and some decent company.

When Dad walked back in some time later, Kat was standing in the kitchen.

"Holy cow!" he exclaimed. "You're going to have to beat the boys away with a stick. You gals did a mighty fine job of turning my sidekick into some kind of a fashion model. What am I going to do now?"

He was very proud of Kat, and knew that he had not been able to give her the upbringing that he would have liked to. He found his camera and they took pictures of everyone with Kat. He had had no idea that his red haired, freckle faced daughter could look like the elegant young lady that stood in front of him.

"Time to go," said Brenda, looking at her watch.

Kat noticed that both Brenda and Nika were wearing matching Rolex watches, but Nika never let hers show. When she asked about them, they told her that they were the milestone awards that they had given themselves when they sold their millionth barrel of oil. Brenda told her that was the day that she had quit worrying. She had mortgaged everything to drill that first well, and had promised herself she would never forget her humble beginnings.

All four of them piled into the cab of the Old Brockle, with Nika at the wheel, to go to the airport. It belched to life with a cloud of blue smoke, and Nika had a bit of trouble with the clutch again. After a few jerks and stalls, they were on their way.

Kat had only flown with Gramps' old friend, Bob, in his Supercub. They used to fly around the farms and over to the edge of the mountains. Bob would let her have the controls at times, and Kat loved it. She had never flown on an airliner before, though, and thought that it would be fun. She asked the lady at the check-in counter for a window seat, so she would not miss a thing.

Kat hugged her dad and new friends good-bye and yelled, "See you in a week," as she disappeared around a corner and out of sight.

"My little tomboy is growing up," Dad said.

"She's a stunning young lady," said Nika. "You're going to have to get used to it. She's growing up on you."

"I made sure that she took a phone card and a bank card with her. She'll be fine," said Brenda as they left the airport. What she did not tell them was that she had secretly made a deposit into Kat's bank account. She did not often have the opportunity to help out anybody who did not ask for it, and truly appreciated Kat as a friend. She liked Kat, and wanted to make certain that she had the opportunity to get an education and see the world.

Kat watched her surroundings closely as she walked down the long hallway to the security check. She waited patiently in line, until they waved her through the metal detector. The buzzers started squealing, as a woman stepped in front of her and motioned her over.

The woman waved a funny looking wand around her arms and legs, and finally stopped at Kat's chest, with the thing beeping loudly. "What's that?" she said bluntly, pointing at Kat's chest.

Kat was not sure what she meant, and was tempted to crack a joke, but thought better of it. The woman standing in front of her looked like she had never smiled in her life, and was not about to start now. Kat took out the tiny medicine bag that Iris had given her, hanging on a buckskin thong around her neck.

The woman looked glumly and said, "Open it."

Kat unfastened the tiny button that held it closed and took out the large gold nugget. The security woman looked in the bag and grunted. Kat assumed that the grunt meant that she was free to proceed so she turned and walked down the hallway.

The man at the United States Customs desk beckoned Kat ahead, and asked her name politely. She told him her name and address. She used the address of the ranch, because she did not really have a place of her own yet. Soon, though, she thought to herself.

"Are you any relation to Maxwell Townsend?" the agent asked.

"Yes, he was my grandfather." Kat answered, not sure why he would ask such a question.

"You be sure to have an exciting week in Las Vegas, and good luck," he said, as he waved her on.

Kat sat down on an uncomfortable bench in the Departures gate area. She soon became bored, so she bought a cup of coffee and stood watching the planes coming and going. She found it hard to believe that her mom had worked as a flight attendant but she herself had never set foot on an airliner.

She wondered how her chauffeurs were making out, on their trip back to the country. Nika had not quite mastered the use of the clutch yet, so every time she took off with the Old Brockle was an experience.

Nika and Brenda had packed her a carry-on bag and had made her promise that she would not peek in it until she was through customs. She decided that it was time for a look, so she went over to a quiet corner and unzipped the flap.

The little bag almost burst when she opened it. It was crammed with books and fashion magazines. A new digital camera lay in the bottom, along with a small, fashionable purse with a long leather strap. The purse contained makeup and the pockets were stuffed with money.

Kat could not believe that these two women whom she had only just met were so good to her. She promised herself that she would always be there for them if they needed her help.

A small note was tucked in a corner pocket. It read, "Bon voyage, Kat. Signed, Honkey and Buster." Kat laughed as she read the note, and was still smiling when her boarding call was announced.

Kat found her seat on the plane and sat down. As she was looking out the window at the runway, an old lady sat down in the seat next to her. Kat watched carefully as the flaps raised and lowered, knowing that the pilot was going through his checks. The plane turned onto the runway. The turbines began to roar and they were off.

The airliner banked around the city and climbed into the clear sky. She could see the snow-covered mountains glistening below, with threads of silver running in the valleys. The roads made a grid of squares, while the irrigation pivots had marked circles in the fields during the past summer. She saw small planes flying at what seemed like a snail's pace, far below them.

The old lady sat patiently until they were levelled out. She looked critically at Kat and asked, "Is this your first trip to Las Vegas?"

"Yes," Kat answered, "I've never been there before."

"You're in for a surprise," said the woman. "There's no other place like it. I've been going down there for years. But you don't look old enough to gamble."

"No," Kat replied, "I'm not old enough to gamble for a year or so. I'm just going for a look around."

The old woman thought for a minute and said, "You won't have much excitement if you can't gamble. That's what Las Vegas is all about."

"Well," Kat replied, "I'm sure I'll find something to do. There's got to be some people that don't gamble there."

"I'm not sure," the woman said, "All the action is in the casinos."

The flight attendants brought drinks and food steadily. You sure won't starve on one of these flights, Kat thought to herself, as she looked in her carry on bag for something to read. She picked out a travel magazine and began to read. She read an article about the "Mayan Riviera" with its all-inclusive resorts. The scuba diving and snorkelling pictures were amazing. Kat decided she would try diving in the ocean one day. She loved animals, and to swim with a giant sea turtle or a dolphin would be something to remember

She thought she would go see the Mayan ruins at Tulum and Chichen Itza. The Mayans had built a huge observatory there, so their knowledge of the stars was incredible. In later years, their culture had become very sadistic, using human sacrifices for their rituals. Kat found this very hard to understand, so she decided to go there some day so she may be able to understand them. The giant pyramid at Chichen Itza had been restored, and the shadows on the stairs looked like a huge writhing snake during the equinox. Kat studied the pictures and read the entire article with interest.

Kat read about islands where people lived as they had a thousand years ago. The tribes there still dressed as they always had. Other islands were now the homes of luxury resorts, with spas and fine dining. Kat thought she preferred the unspoiled islands, where nature still prevailed. She could not help thinking of the Bella Coola Valley, where the ecology was so fragile that it could very easily be spoiled forever.

Kat's ears began popping as the plane made its decent from the sky. She put her things away and looked out the window at the desert below. It was far different than she had imagined it to be. In the movies, she had seen the deserts consisting of soft blowing sand for miles, but the ground below her was rough and rugged. Very little grew on the land because it was so dry, but what there was looked thorny and uninviting.

Kat saw the large desert city as they made their final approach, and then felt the plane touch the runway. The pilot braked hard and pulled the plane up to the terminal.

Kat waited patiently as people gathered up their things and filed off the plane. A tour guide led them down to the carousel to pick up their luggage. Kat pulled her designer luggage off and carried it to a waiting bus.

She could not believe how warm it was outside. When she had left home a few hours ago, it was twenty degrees below zero. She did not even need a jacket here. She loaded her luggage into a compartment under the bus and walked up the steps. The driver asked which hotel she was staying at and Kat replied, "Caesar's Palace," as she sat down.

She followed the people who got off at her hotel to the check-in counter, and stood in line until she got to the counter. Brenda had told her what to do and say, but she was a bit uncertain. She handed her room voucher to the lady at the desk and waited.

The woman studied it and checked her computer. She handed Kat a folder with a credit card in it and said, "Room 629, elevators are over there. Sixth floor, to your left."

Kat took the folder and wheeled her luggage into the elevator. She pressed six and up she went. When the elevator stopped, she went left until she found room 629.

Kat could not figure out why they had not given her a key, but saw there was no keyhole in the door. She read the instructions on the door, and found that the credit card had to be put into the slotted mechanism by the handle.

She took the card and put it in the slot but when she tried the handle it still would not turn. She turned the card this way and that way, until she was ready to give up, when a voice behind her startled her.

THE MUSHROOM PICKER

"Having trouble? Maybe I can help you," the voice said. Kat turned around and came face to face with a dark skinned man.

"I can't get this silly thing to work," said Kat. "I've never used one of these before."

The young man took the card and swiped it through the lock. When the light turned green, he opened the door. He held the card out, and showed her which way it went and how to use it. Kat was embarrassed at being so naïve.

"My name is Kanoa," said the boy. "If you have any trouble, just knock on the door across the hall."

"Mine's Kat, short for Kathy," Kat said. "I'll probably come knocking. I'm from a ranch in Canada, so I'm not used to city life."

"I'm from Hawaii, and it's my first time away from the islands, so Las Vegas is new for me too."

"Why would you leave Hawaii to come here?" asked Kat. "Isn't it supposed to be like paradise?"

"It is paradise, Kat," he replied. "I want to see what the rest of the world is like, though. Actually, I had to come with my aunties. My Mom was supposed to come with them, but she got sick and made me take her place."

"I understand," said Kat. "I want to travel too."

"You should come to Hawaii," said Kanoa. "I teach surfing at Waikiki. I'd be glad to teach you."

"I'd love that. Maybe one of these days I'll take you up on your offer."

"Hey Kat, I promised to take my aunties dancing this evening. Would you like to come along? It won't be much of a date with the aunties there, but I will try to make the best of it."

Kat thought about it for a minute. This was the first time she had been asked out in a long while. She felt sure Kanoa was a good guy, and besides, the aunties would be there, whoever they were. "Okay, what time?" she asked.

"I'll knock on your door at eight," Kanoa replied, and went to his room.

Kat unlocked her door expertly and walked into her luxurious room. She lay down on her bed and fell sound asleep.

When she woke up, she was starving. She went downstairs and found a snack bar where she could buy a hot dog and a Coke.

The sound of bells ringing attracted her, as a giant door swung open. Kat walked into the casino, and realized that what people had told her was absolutely true.

There was row upon row of slot machines, with bells ringing and lights flashing. Progressive numbers climbed higher and higher, while people sat pulling the handles, hoping for the big win. People circled around the roulette wheels and crap tables, while the dealers handled hundreds of chips, passing them back and forth as the players set them on the tables and won or lost.

The card tables were quieter, but the chips still moved back and forth. An old woman bumped into Kat, and she noticed that the woman was carrying a small pail full of silver dollars. These people play for some big stakes, she thought.

A woman jumped up from her stool and screamed like a bee had stung her on the rump, but when Kat walked by where she was standing, she noticed that the woman had won a bunch of nickels. Kat went back to her room to get ready for her date.

Kat was ready to go when Kanoa came to the door. His aunties were waiting in the hallway.

"Kat, this is my Auntie Kailani and Auntie Akela. They'll be our chaperones for tonight. Aunties, this is Kathy Townsend, she'll be my date tonight." They all laughed as they headed down the hall.

"Gilley's Saloon and Dance Hall," said Kanoa, when they were all in the taxi. The driver gunned it, and they flew through the traffic like mad. Kat just hung on for dear life, fearful that each breath she took might be her last.

Kanoa was out of the door before the taxi had stopped completely. He held the door for the ladies, and helped each of them out. When they got into the dance hall, he found them a table, and held their chairs as each of them sat down.

"What a gentleman," Kat thought. "The only other guy that's so polite is my Dad." She ordered a coke and waited for the music to start.

"Are you a surfer, Kathy?" asked Auntie Akela.

"No, I'm from Canada. I've never even seen the surf, but one day I will."

"I thought maybe you got those scars from the reef," said Auntie. "Most of us Hawaiians have them from wipe-outs. The surf pulls you down onto the coral and it cuts you to ribbons."

"I got these from a grizzly bear," said Kat.

THE MUSHROOM PICKER

"You must have been very scared," said Auntie Kailani.

"Yes, I was," Kat answered. "I was up on the mountain by myself, but it wasn't as bad as you may think. My Grandfather taught me how to survive in the woods."

"Is there snow where you come from?" asked Auntie Kailani. "I've only seen it on television."

"Oh, yeah," Kat replied. "The ranch is covered in snow. It will stay around until April."

"Isn't that something? We get a bit of rain and wind at times. Kanoa likes it when it blows, because the waves are higher. He lives in the ocean on that surfboard of his. Sometimes I worry about him."

"Oh, Auntie, there's nothing like riding a big wave or surfing in the pipe. It's the best thrill a guy will ever have," said Kanoa.

The band began to play, so their conversation was drowned out. Kat grabbed Kanoa and dragged him onto the dance floor.

"I don't know how to do this," Kanoa moaned.

"Just follow my lead," said Kat. "Relax and I'll teach you."

They danced awkwardly around the floor, with Kanoa trying much too hard, so he almost stumbled at times. Kat tried hard not to laugh when the song ended. She looked at Kanoa and chuckled, "I can't believe you can ride a surfboard on a wave but can't stand up on a dance floor."

Kanoa was a quick learner. By the time a few songs played, he was two-stepping like a true cowboy. When Kat sat down, he got Auntie Kailani onto the dance floor to show off his new skill.

"Are you Kanoa's mom's sisters?" Kat asked his Auntie Akela.

"Oh no, dear, we just work with his mom. In Hawaii, all of the young people call the older women Auntie. It's just a way to show respect for their elders."

"That's nice," Kat said, as the music cut her off.

The band began playing a country line dance and Akela hauled Kat to the dance floor. Akela lined up beside Kailani and Kanoa and hollered, "Let's do the Huki Lau!"

They had a few drinks in them and were out to have fun. They began to do a hula dance that Kat had never seen. The three of them moved in unison with smooth and flowing motions. The line dancers finally noticed them, and moved to the side to watch. They put on such a show that everyone clapped and yelled, "Encore!" when the song ended.

They danced to one more song, then sat down amid a huge round of applause. The waiters brought a tray of drinks from the other customers to show their appreciation.

"Where did you learn to dance like that?" Kat asked.

"We learn to hula when we are very young," said Akela. "Kanoa could dance the Huki Lau when he was three. We all dance at the luaus at times. It's part of life on the islands."

"Someday, I'm going to learn the Huki Lau and ride a surfboard," said Kat.

They spent the rest of the evening talking and dancing, until Akela said, "We have to fly home in a few hours. We'd better go back and sleep for a couple of hours."

The taxi ride back was as terrifying as the ride to the dance hall. The casino was just as busy as it had been in the daytime.

Akela unlocked their door and dragged Kanoa into their room. As Kat was unlocking her door, he ran back and gave her a big kiss, then raced back and pretended not to hear the scolding his Aunties were giving him.

Kat walked into her room and crawled into bed. She wondered if she would ever see any of them again. Kanoa had given her his E-mail address so she could send him a note when he got home.

The maid was already making up Kanoa's room when Kat stepped into the hallway the next morning. Kat felt a touch of loneliness, which was unusual for her. She had always been a loner, comfortable on her own.

She walked into the street, where people walked by the hundreds from one casino to the next. "All these people and not a friend among them," Kat thought as she walked. "Maybe I'm just not accustomed to the city life."

Two greasy young men in baggy clothes came up from behind her. Suddenly her purse was wrenched from her shoulder, and one of them raced away with it. When she went to sprint after it, the second guy tripped her, and she fell to the sidewalk, while he disappeared into the crowd. When Kat got up, they were gone, and she had no idea where they would be. She walked slowly back to her hotel.

When Kat got back to her room she checked her safe to make sure her bank card and plane ticket were still there. She had most of her cash in there as well. Nika had warned her about carrying that much cash and she was glad she had taken her advice.

Kat was furious. That pair of useless bums had her money and driver's license. She knew that it would be useless to call the police. They were much too busy to investigate petty thefts.

Kat turned on the television but did not pay any attention. She lay on her bed and fell asleep.

The television was still on when Kat woke up in the afternoon. She felt uncomfortable and alone. She had not rested very much during her fitful sleep. Kat went to find something to eat.

She headed down the Strip, going into one casino after another. She stopped at a deli to buy a sandwich and a Coke. She watched the people go back and forth, trying to win their fortune. There were people of all ages and lifestyles. She was beginning to be able to pick out the tourists. There was something different about them.

She was not in a hurry. She was beginning to think that the old woman on the plane was right, that her trip might be boring. She decided to make her way up the Strip until she was tired, then she could take a taxi back to the hotel. Time was not a factor, because this town did not slow down, day or night.

Kat walked from one casino to the next, taking in every sight they had to offer. She had not realized that many of the casinos had different collections of cars, guns and other objects on exhibit.

It was dark when she arrived at Circus Circus. The lights in the front of the casinos were flashing, making the Strip into one giant machine. A trapeze act was just beginning as Kat walked into the circus area. How those girls could fly through the air and the men could catch them was a mystery to Kat. She thought the circus people must be underpaid for the amount they risked their lives.

Kat watched a couple of acts before she moved on. She went up the next floor to the arcade. She tried some of the arcade games and each time she won, she would get a stuffed toy that she would give to one of the little kids beside her.

She was trying to pick up a stuffed toy with a flimsy grapple, when a middle-aged man came up and started to play the one beside her. She won several toys while he did not get any, and she saw him stop and decide to just watch her.

"You're good," he said, as Kat decided that she had played enough.

"I've seen enough for one day," Kat said.

"Are you waiting for someone?" the man asked.

"No, I'm just going to take a taxi back to my hotel."

"No need to do that," the man said. "I'll give you a ride. My car's just outside."

"That's all right," said Kat. "I can just take a cab."

"I insist," the man said. "It's part of the hospitality of Las Vegas. I'd be glad to drop you off."

"Well, if you insist, but I sure don't want to impose," said Kat.

THE MUSHROOM PICKER

"Follow me. I'm sorry, I haven't even introduced myself. My name's Nick."

"I'm Kat."

She followed Nick out of the casino to his car. Nick unlocked the black convertible and they hopped in. Nick started the car and had backed out when his flip phone rang. The music was loud so Kat heard nothing of his conversation. He seemed to be upset about something when he finished.

"That was my wife," he said. "The baby's crying and I have to bring her some milk. It's just a few blocks out of the way over to Caesar's. You can meet the wife."

Kat really did not want to go meet Nick's family. She was dressed in her "Grizzly" sweatshirt with a picture of a roaring bear on the front, jeans and sneakers. Nick did not seem to care, though. He said his wife did not care how people dressed. They turned off the Strip and drove to a nice house in a residential area.

"You may as well come in and see the baby," said Nick, opening her door like a true gentleman. "They say he looks like me."

Nick unlocked the door and motioned for Kat to go into the house as he followed. As soon as she was in the house, he turned around and locked the door behind him, and put the key into his pocket. Then he turned around and said, "You're mine now, baby."

He walked to the counter and took out a small container from a drawer. Then he poured some powder onto the counter and sucked it up his nose. He gulped a huge swig of vodka to wash it down.

Kat tried the door, but it was locked with the key and would not open. She knew she was in trouble. Kat tried to think of a way to escape, but her mind was numb.

"Stupid!" She said to herself. "You're just plain stupid."

Nick turned around and sniffed. "Want some?" he said.

"No," Kat replied. "Don't use the stuff."

"I'm gonna teach you to like it, Scarface. In a couple weeks you'll be begging me for it, but I've got bigger plans for you first. Tonight we're gonna have us some fun."

Nick walked over and tore Kat's sweatshirt from her body. He was a big man who appeared to be extremely strong.

Kat knew that she had to keep her mind clear, and now was no time for emotion. She noticed that the place was messy. Women's clothing was scattered all over the floor. There was no furniture except an ornate king sized bed in the corner. She could not see the bedrooms down the hall.

"He's a bloody pimp," Kat thought to herself. "Boy, am I stupid."

Nick sucked more cocaine up his nose, and drank another slug from the bottle. He walked around the room, sneering an evil grin.

"I've got me some clients who's gonna love having you. They gonna like them scars on your back. Let 'em know you like the rough stuff. They'll pay top dollar for you, Red."

Kat just looked down at the floor, secretly peeking around the room. There were empty pizza boxes and Styrofoam take out containers everywhere, but no weapons.

Kat felt for Gramps' old jackknife in her pocket to insure it was still there. It was a last resort, though. If she pulled it out, she would probably have to kill him.

Kat spotted a pair of handcuffs, partially concealed by some clothing, just as Nick walked over, kicked her, and threw her onto the bed. He laughed and walked around the corner to the bathroom.

Kat grabbed the handcuffs and slipped them into the back of her jeans. She unlaced one shoe and made a loop with a slipknot in one end, which she fed into her pocket.

Nick walked back into the room buck-naked. He sniffed some more cocaine and finished the vodka. He sneered an evil smile as he peered at her through glazed eyes.

"I'm gonna give you lesson number one tonight, and tomorrow you're gonna get stoned, then you're gonna need me and be my property."

Kat noticed that Nick was beginning to slur his words. When he walked towards her, he stumbled a bit, which may give her the split second advantage she needed. The windows were barred so she would have to somehow get the key from his pocket. She had a plan but would have to act fast.

Nick walked over and put his huge hands on the bed for support. Kat flew into action. She snapped one cuff around his wrist and pulled hard to throw him off balance.

As he fell, she snapped the other cuff around the metal bedpost. As he swung at her with his free hand, she grabbed it and pulled it back behind him while slipping the looped shoelace over his free wrist. She let go against his struggling, and his arm snapped forward. She whipped the free end of the shoelace around the other bedpost and tied it tightly in a half hitch.

Kat was glad Gramps had taught her how to use her shoelaces. He had always told her, "Throw those new shoelaces away and buy the strongest ones money can buy. They may save your life someday. Remember what they can do for you, Kat."

Nick kicked and screamed, trying to get free, but he was there to stay.

"Unlock me! The key is over there on the counter. I'll kill you if you don't unlock me right now. I'll call my friend and we will all have a go at you. You won't move for a month. Let me loose, you little bitch!" He yelled over and over.

Nick was tied face down so he had to cross his arms to look up. He would try to pull loose, only to just fall back. His words became more slurred, and his eyes bulged, as the drugs and booze fought each other for control of his brain.

Kat found the key for the handcuffs, and held it up for Nick to see. He resumed his rage until he began to foam at the mouth.

Kat found where Nick had left his clothes, and took the door key from his pocket. She walked back to where he was ranting on the bed.

"Shut up!" she said, as she began to lecture him about his evil deeds. She waved her finger in his face as he cursed her, while she thought about what the fisherman had said to the guy at Bella Coola, "He was shaking his finger in the guy's face so hard I thought he was going to take his eye out."

Kat stood back and looked closely at Nick, knowing there would be other girls after her if she let him get away with this. She slowly drew Gramps' old pocket knife from her pocket as she glared at Nick, lying helplessly on the bed. He cursed her and kicked at her, until she opened the middle blade and ran her thumb over it to test the edge. Then the look in his eyes turned from hatred to horror, and the veins stood out on his face.

He cried and screamed, as he begged her not to do it.

"I'd be doing the world a favor," was all she said.

She decided not to, because she would spend a long time in jail and that was not for her. She would just scare the daylights out of him. She touched his thigh with the back side of the blade and Nick fainted.

Kat searched through the clothes on the floor until she found a lacy top to replace her torn sweatshirt. It was low cut, front and back, but it was the least transparent garment in the room. Nick's cell phone rang a few times as she tied her old Grizzly sweatshirt around her waist.

She knew that Nick had to be caught for what he was doing, and devised a plan. She untied Nick and wiped away her fingerprints from anything she may have touched, then she pulled the flimsy covers over Nick so it looked like he had been sleeping. She picked up his cell phone and dialled 911.

Kat wiped her prints from the phone, and then placed it in Nick's right hand. After a quick look around the room to make sure there was nothing left that may place her there, she pressed the "Send" button and raced out the door.

Kat was in good shape, so she sprinted for several blocks. She could already hear the sirens wailing, and presumed they were going to Nick's house. Somebody had told her once that the fire department could track a cell phone, but she was not certain.

A car came down the street, so Kat stepped back into the shadows. She stepped on something, and almost tripped. When she picked it up, she saw that it was a street hockey stick that some kids must have left. Gramps would have liked this one for a cow chaser, she thought to herself.

The wooden handle was covered with fibreglass to make it stronger, and well taped, with a ball at the end so it would not slip out of the player's hands. The blade of the hockey stick was just broken off. Kat decided she would use it for a walking stick, because her leg hurt where Nick had kicked her. She felt a lot safer carrying the stick.

Kat pressed on through the unfamiliar city, not sure how to get back to her hotel. She found a box on the street corner with free advertising on it, and on the back of one of the flyers there was a map of Las Vegas. Kat checked the street signs above her to find where she was.

Police flew past her with their lights and sirens on. Each time Kat saw one, she would step back into the darkness to make herself invisible. She had had enough excitement for one night.

Kat was much further from the Strip than she had originally thought. It had not seemed far in Nick's convertible. She followed the streets that she found on the map, until she finally saw the lights of the Strip. She began to relax, knowing that she was almost to familiar territory.

Don was cruising, a block away from the Strip, when he saw the hooker. He had been a police officer for over twenty years and could spot them.

This one was new in town. She walked with a slight limp, and was carrying a walking stick. Don wondered who had made the scars that ran down her back above the low cut hooker outfit.

He felt sorry for those girls. They would begin as confused young girls, but by the time their pimps got them working, they would be hooked on crack, with no place to go.

He was tired and ready to go off shift. He had listened to the excitement that his co-workers had had from a 911 call earlier. They had found so much stuff that his sergeant had called for radio silence. He would no doubt find out in a few days, when he went back to work, but right now he just wanted his days off that started in an hour.

He pulled the police cruiser over, putting the spotlight on Kat. She scolded herself for not having seen this one coming from behind.

Kat turned around and squinted into the blinding light. The officer got out and told her to approach the car. He asked her if she had any needles or weapons.

"No," said Kat. "Just an old jackknife."

He watched her as she took it out and set it on the hood of the car.

"What's that?" he asked, pointing to her neck.

"It's my medicine bag," Kat replied.

"Show me what is inside," he said, assuming that it was crack cocaine.

Kat carefully opened the little bag and pulled out the shiny gold nugget. Don took it into his hand and studied it.

"Where'd you get it?" he asked.

"I found it on the side of a mountain in British Columbia."

THE MUSHROOM PICKER

"What is your name and address and what are you doing in Las Vegas?" he asked.

Kat told him how she had came to be in Las Vegas, and that she was just out for a walk. He was beginning to believe her, but still could not figure out why she would dress like that. Maybe Canadian girls were different. She definitely was not a hooker, but there was sure something odd about her.

He watched her limp away, and drove around the block, where he parked the cruiser to follow on foot for a couple of blocks. If she were up to something, he would soon find out. If she were bringing trouble to his beat, she would soon find herself downtown behind bars.

Kat saw two scruffy looking people emerge from the construction site far ahead of her, but they disappeared into the distance. As she got closer, she saw two men hanging around the construction area. She immediately recognized them as the fellows who had robbed her on the street. One was tall and lean, with long stringy hair, while the other was stocky, with a toque on his head. Kat had a score to settle with them and walked straight into the vacant lot.

Don watched Kat walk into the lot, and thought that he had finally solved the mystery that had been bothering him. The red haired girl was a drug runner. He hid in the shadows and waited for them to do the exchange. When the drugs changed hands, he would arrest all three of them. He recognized the two thugs as petty criminals from the area, who belonged to one of the local gangs. He drew his revolver from its holster and waited.

Kat walked up to the men and said, "Hey, you pair of piss ants, give me back my money."

They both looked at her and laughed. "You're stupid, girl, we gonna have a little fun with you." The tall man clutched at Kat, who spun around and clubbed him on the side of the knee. He went down in pain. The stocky one laughed at him as he tried to grab Kat. She hit him on the knee as hard as she could with the hockey stick.

Don could not believe what he was seeing. He would have to stop it when the girl was in danger, but these punks deserved every blow they were taking. He was not sure if the little red haired girl was trained or just lucky.

He saw the tall one pull a knife from his baggy pants and raised his pistol to shoot, but Kat was in the crossfire.

Kat saw the flicker of the knife, and brought the stick down hard across the punk's forearm. He dropped the knife and screamed in pain.

The short one tried to kick Kat with his heavy boot but felt the stick hit his jaw hard. He pulled his knife, only to have it knocked from his hand.

Don soon realized that the girl was a trained fighter. It was as though she had rehearsed the entire fight, and was in complete control. He had not seen the punks land a single blow yet, even though they were twice her size. He was surprised that they had not run away in fear yet, but they probably did not realize that they were being beaten that badly.

Don decided that he had pegged the little redhead wrong. He kept his gun in his hand, ready to fire should he need to.

The men kept trying to kick and hit Kat, but she hit them with blow after blow. She saw the tall man's hand drop to his side, followed by a glint of steel.

"Game over, you piss ants," Kat said, as she flew at them.

When Don saw the man pull out the gun, he prepared to fire, but the girl leaped between them and into the crossfire. As the gun came up, Kat hit his hand with a drive that could have won the World Series. Don saw the gun rattle across the ground and saw the man's fingers splay out in all directions. The girl then raised the stick high, and said something that Don could not hear. She went at them both, hitting them with blow after blow. They tried to protect themselves with their arms, but she would just hit them in the ribs so their arms would drop. When they tried to turn away she would hit them even harder, so they were forced to face her.

Maybe she will teach them a lesson, Don thought.

"Don't knock them down until you're darned sure they won't get up again," Gramps had always said, as he stood there in his old, tattered cowboy hat watching her every move. "Then knock them down hard!"

Kat watched to make sure she was wearing them down. They fought back less and less, until she decided it was time to take them down. She wanted her money back, and was not about to let them go until she had it. They had twenty dollars of her money and her driver's license.

She clubbed them both on the kneecaps a few times to make sure they could not run after her and, when she was ready for them to go down, she held her stick like a spear. She drove the tall one in the chest with her spear and he dropped like a stone. The short one turned to run so she clubbed him on the side of the knee and speared him in the chest as he spun around.

"Give me my money and my driver's license back!" Kat said from her position of power above them. She held the broken hockey stick high above them. "And toss that gun," she said to the short one.

"Two fingers," she said, as he lifted the pistol from his pocket and tossed it. She held the club like a Roman Gladiator, poised for the kill.

The men reached in their pockets, and pulled out wads of money and cards that Kat stuffed into her pockets.

"Face the ground and don't look up for an hour. If you do, I'll belt you a good one," Kat said. She gave each of them a hard one on the rump to drive the point home.

Kat picked up the guns and knives before she walked away. A large pipe from a piling protruded from the ground in the construction area. Kat dropped the weapons down the pipe as she walked by, and listened as they landed far below. She looked back to see that the men had not moved. They lay still, like children playing hide and seek. She walked onto the sidewalk and turned toward the lights of the Strip.

Don walked back to the cruiser and pulled back onto the street. He watched as the little red haired girl, with scars covering her naked back, limped slowly down the sidewalk. She used the broken hockey stick to help her along. He knew now that he had made an enormous error in judging her, and could not help but wonder what she was doing here.

He pulled the cruiser up beside her and asked her to get in. "Where are you staying?" he asked.

"At Caesar's Palace," she answered tiredly.

"Is anybody with you?"

"No, I'm staying alone," Kat said.

"Those were some dangerous men you beat back there. I'm sure they won't admit to being beaten by you, but they could sneak up on you. That's the way they operate. Would you consider staying at my house tonight?"

Kat was far too tired to resist, so she just said, "Sure, if it's okay with you."

They drove to Caesar's Palace, and Don escorted Kat to her room and waited while she gathered up her things and packed her suitcase.

"I just have to stop at the station to check out, and then we can go to my house. By the way, my name's Don," the officer said, as they drove down the Strip.

They stopped at the station and went in. Kat had never been in a police station before, and did not realize how busy they were late at night. Don brought Kat a cup of fresh coffee that tasted mighty good to her.

"Quiet night, Don?" an officer asked, as they walked by.

"Yeah, pretty quiet. How about you?"

"Yeah, my beat was quiet, but some of the guys are still out on that radio silence one. I guess we'll find out about it tomorrow."

"I'm starting my days off," said Don. "Guess I'll hear all about it when I get back."

Don led Kat to a small office and sat down in front of the computer. "What did you say your last name was, Kat?"

"Townsend. Kathy Townsend."

He tapped more keys and asked, "Any relation to Max Townsend?"

"Yes, he was my Gramps. Why do you ask?"

"Your Gramps has security clearance second only to the president himself. We wouldn't even be able to detain him or impede his progress in any way. What did he do, Kat? I've never even met anybody with clearance like that"

"He was just my Gramps," she answered. "He was an old rancher on the edge of the Canadian Rockies. He taught me most everything I know."

"How to fight with a broken hockey stick?" Don asked.

"Yes, he sure did that," Kat smiled. "He'd make me practice until I had blisters on my hands."

"That explains a lot," Don said, as he typed more. He decided that Kat's grandfather must have been a special agent for the United States, for which department he was not sure. He must have trained his granddaughter in special combat. That was why she could fight against those thugs. It was the most exciting, most one-sided battle that he had ever seen. He would be worried about taking on those two, even with a gun in his hand.

D on looked a lot less imposing when he came out wearing a Mickey Mouse sweatshirt and blue jeans. They went out and got into an old blue Chrysler.

"They don't make them like this any more," said Don. "This used to be my dad's car. I got it when he passed away."

They drove to a small house on the edge of the city. Kat was extremely careful and waited until Don opened the door wide and walked in before she entered the house. She looked around, and saw that the house was well kept, with family pictures hanging on the wall.

A woman sat up on the couch, putting down a book that she was reading. She stood up, walked over, and gave Don a big hug. He said, "Kathy, this is my wife Pat. Pat, this is Kathy Townsend. She is going to stay with us tonight."

Pat thought it was strange that Don would bring somebody home with him. He seldom talked about his work, and had never brought anybody home with him in over twenty years. However, she trusted his judgement, even though the girl had scars on her face and back and dressed like a hooker. She decided to bite her tongue and make the girl feel at home.

"Where are you from, Kathy?" she asked.

"I'm Canadian," said Kat. "I grew up in Alberta, but I've been on the Pacific Coast for the past few months, living with a Native family."

"Sounds like you travel quite a bit," said Pat.

"Not really," Kat replied. "This was my first time on a plane."

Pat set out snacks and tea, and Kat realized that she had not eaten for hours. She had to restrain herself from eating everything on the coffee table. When she sat down after pouring more tea, she felt the money in her pocket, and remembered that she had only stopped at the hotel long enough to pack. She looked down at her clothes and was completely embarrassed.

"I'm sorry. I don't normally dress like this, but it was all I could find," Kat said, hoping she had not said too much. She dug in her pockets and pulled out the wads of money and the cards she had rescued from the punks.

Pat looked surprised, but Kat was too exhausted for anything to shock her. She took twenty dollars from the pile of cash, and found her driver's license. Then she pushed the pile of money over to Don.

"Keep it," he said. "I'll turn the cards in, but we'll never find whose money that is."

"I don't want it," Kat said. "How about I give it to charity? I'll look around and find a good home for it."

"Sounds great," both Don and Pat replied.

Kat felt the scars on her face ache. They got sore whenever she was extremely tired. "Could I borrow an aspirin, please?" Kat asked Pat. "These scars hurt when I get tired."

"Sure," Pat answered, as she went to find some.

"I don't want to pry," said Pat when she returned, handing her the two aspirins, "but how did you get those scars?"

Kat told her about the bear attack and the trip down the mountain. They sat wide-eyed, asking her questions whenever she stopped talking. When she finished, Don said, "Kathy, I have to apologize. I judged you completely wrong when I first saw you on the street. I thought you were a hooker, but you've proven me very wrong."

Kat laughed and said, "No harm done. I'm glad you were there. I'm sure glad you brought me to your house. I wouldn't have slept very well at the hotel and thank you, Pat, for having me."

Kat leaned back and relaxed as Don and Pat talked between themselves. When they looked back she was sound asleep. Don picked her up, surprisingly small in sleep, and carried her to the spare bedroom, where Pat tucked her in

"Tell me about her," Pat asked Don, as she crawled into bed.

"I'm not sure what to tell you, Pat," Don said. "I thought she was a new hooker in town when I saw her first, but she's anything but a hooker. I watched her beat two of the toughest punks on the Strip to within an inch of their lives tonight with a broken hockey stick. She even stripped them of their knives and guns. I couldn't get a shot away, and just had to watch. She didn't need my help anyway. She's from Canada. Her grandfather was a fighter and she learned well. That's about all I can tell you."

"She seems very nice," said Pat. "At first I was wondering what you were dragging home, but I kind of like her."

The drum pounded out a steady beat. Dancers moved silently in a circle, with a salmon and an eagle accompanying them. The giant Grizzly, with Raven on his shoulder, stood at one end. In the centre, Nick lay motionless with his eyes wide open. Kat saw the scarred young woman with arrowheads at the end of each of her braids. As she looked around, she saw that all the dancers had the scars of the bear's great claws. When she danced to the front of the circle in front of the bear, the drumming stopped. She looked straight into the bear's eyes as he nodded his approval. She was so comfortable here. The dancers all looked straight at her and nodded. No words were spoken between them. When she danced in front of the giant bear again, he roared like thunder, "Go back."

Kat woke up in a strange bed. She recalled the dream as though she had just walked away from the place. She walked to the door and looked around. She was still in Don and Pat's house, safe and sound. Kat went back to bed and fell sound asleep.

A little girl was sitting on her bed, reading a book, when Kat awakened. She noticed that the girl was holding the book upside down, and chuckled. The little girl spoke as soon as she noticed that Kat was awake.

"My name is Lindsay, what's yours?" she asked.

"My name is Kat," she answered.

"Is that why you have scratches on your face?" the little one asked, not waiting for an answer. "My Grandma sent you this." She dragged a housecoat onto the bed.

Kat put the housecoat on, as Lindsay dragged her from the room. Pat and Don were sitting in the kitchen having toast and coffee.

"Did she wake you up?" asked Pat.

"No," Kat answered. "She was reading a book when I woke up."

"And I can't even read yet," said Lindsay proudly.

"Kat, this is our granddaughter, Lindsay," said Pat.

"We've already met," Kat said cheerfully.

Kat had coffee and toast, while Lindsay ran around the house playing with her toys. "Can you dance?" she asked Kat, as she raced toward her.

"Sure," Kat replied. "I can do the two-step."

"Show me how," said Lindsay. Kat placed Lindsay's feet on hers and danced around the living room, hanging on to her. Pat put on a country tune and they all laughed and laughed.

"Do you know any different ones?" asked Lindsay.

"I just learned the Huki Lau but I'm not very good at it. I'll teach you what I know." Kat went over to Pat's C.D. collection and picked some tunes they could Hula to. She got Lindsay lined up, and they commenced their first Huki Lau lesson.

Kat forgot all about the troubles in her life, and she became a child herself. Don and Pat sat back and watched as the two girls practiced the Huki Lau over and over. Lindsay would not let Kat quit, even though she was only four, and Kat knew she had just made a true friend.

"We've got to take Lindsay back to our daughter's in Reno today, Kat. Would you like to come with us? We'll be gone a few days or so, and it would give you a chance to see a bit more of Nevada," said Pat.

"Please come. Please, please, please," Lindsay begged.

Kat had nothing else on her agenda, so she said, "I'd like that very much. Thanks for the offer." Lindsay raced around the house, cheering.

Don handed Kat an envelope full of bills. "There's over four thousand dollars in there, Kat. Those guys must be big time dealers, and they'll be doin' time as soon as I get back to work, so they won't need it. Find a good home for it, Kat."

"I will," she replied.

Kat could remember the dream from the night before as if it had just happened. She could not understand what it meant, and why Nick was there. It must have just been a wild dream, she thought.

She got dressed and packed her suitcase, which she put in the trunk of the old blue Chrysler. She practiced the Huki Lau a few more times with Lindsay, while Don and Pat got ready for the long trip.

Kat was surprised at how rugged the desert was as they drove through it. The vegetation looked brown and lifeless, not like the bright green that flourished in the Canadian summers. She saw fields of vegetables for the very first time, with Mexican workers bent over weeding in the fields. Kat felt sorry for those people, having to work so hard in the heat. All they had out in the field was an old school bus for transportation, which pulled a portable toilet around. There was the odd herd of skinny cows grazing along the highway. "It would take a thousand acres to feed a few cows in this country. Not much seems to grow around here."

"No, but when it does rain, the desert is beautiful," said Pat. "All of the plants that seem to be dead start to bloom." The old Chrysler rumbled along with Don at the wheel, wishing at times he had his cruiser so that he could pull some of these drivers over and give them a ticket.

Lindsay and Pat sang every song either of them knew. They tried to teach Kat, but she had not heard many of them, and kept getting the words mixed up. Kat taught them a couple of country songs that they both learned quickly. They played games that Lindsay knew. Kat thought that maybe she made up a few of the rules as she played, but it did not matter as long as they were having fun.

Don pulled into a truck stop along the highway to gas up the Chrysler and to get some lunch. Lindsay ate like a trooper. Kat could not believe that a tiny little girl could eat so much. Don looked very proud, Kat thought, travelling with his little family and the waif he had found on the sidewalk. She offered to pay for lunch, but Don insisted on paying. Kat bought a Coke for the road and some candy for Lindsay, before they got back into the comfy old Chrysler. Kat and Lindsay sat in the back seat, and, before long, Lindsay put her head on Kat's lap and fell asleep. Kat was soon to follow.

Kat woke up just in time to see the lights of Reno coming into sight. She felt rested and refreshed, quickly becoming her old self once again. Don drove the shiny vintage car up and down the city streets, until he pulled up in front of an older home. Lindsay woke up as soon as the car stopped and sat up rubbing her eyes.

"You're home, Dear," said Pat quietly, as a young woman walked from the house.

"Mommy!" Lindsay yelled, opening the car door and running to the woman who snatched her up and gave her a big hug. Don and Pat also got a hug from her.

"Connie, this is our new friend, Kathy Townsend. Kat, I'd like to introduce you to our daughter Connie. She's Lindsay's mother."

"Hi, Kathy. Welcome to Reno. I hope you won't mind sharing a room with Lindsay. Our house isn't very big."

"No, I sure don't mind," Kat replied. "We've become good friends, haven't we, Lindsay?"

"Oh yes, Mom," Lindsay yelled. "Kat showed me how to do the Huki Lau," and she began her hula show. They all laughed as they unpacked the car and carried their bags into the house.

"Sam's working nights," said Connie, as they packed their things in.

"That's too bad," Don said. "I was hoping we could do some fishing, but I guess I'll have to go alone."

"Sorry, Dad," Connie said. "He tried to get the time off, but they're short staffed right now, so he's had to cover extra shifts."

Pat explained to Kat that Connie's husband was also a police officer. He was fairly new on the force, so he had to take some shifts that he would rather not have. Kat felt sorry for the man she had never met, for having to leave his little family at night while he went out onto the streets to fight crime.

"Come see my room!" Lindsay said, pulling on Kat's fingers. Kat followed her into the little girl's room, and saw it was decorated with Disney's Little Mermaid. There were Little Mermaid posters on the walls, and ornaments on the dressers.

"See all my Little Mermaids?" said Lindsay. "I watch the Little Mermaid whenever my mom lets me. At Halloween I was a Little Mermaid."

"That's nice," said Kat. "Your mom sure has your room well decorated. When I was a little girl, my grandma decorated a room for me at her house."

Connie rolled a folding bed into the room and made it up for Kat. She was only a few years older than Kat. She asked Kat if she liked to play checkers, because Lindsay would be asking her to play and would not stop until she made her. Kat said that she used to play checkers with Gramps, and liked the game too. Connie said that she had supper ready, so they went down to the kitchen.

Lindsay insisted on sitting beside Kat. As soon as the meal was over, she dragged Kat up to do a Hula show. She was becoming quite the little dancer, Kat thought. Kat had no idea if they were doing it right, but they were having fun.

A man walked through the door, grabbed Lindsay, and spun her around him. Then he gave her a hug and held her out at arm's length. "You've grown a foot," he said.

"Hi Dad," Lindsay said, as soon as she could catch her breath. She slipped her tiny hand into his and pulled him to where Kat was sitting.

"This is my friend Kat, she's going to sleep over with me. She showed me how to do the Huki Lau," she told him, and broke into her much loved Hula. Her father watched, smiling silently, as she gracefully moved her arms while she danced around the floor.

Connie stood beside the man. As soon as Lindsay had finished her dance, she said, "Kat, this is my husband, Sam. Sam, this is Kat. She came over with Mom and Dad. She's staying in Lindsay's room, so I'm sure she'll hear everything there is to know about the Little Mermaid."

"You like checkers, Kat?" Sam asked. "If you don't she'll drive you crazy."

"Oh yeah, I've already been warned."

They sat around the kitchen table, chatting about the young couple's life in Reno. Sam had called in to tell his dispatcher that he was taking an hour off, so their visit would have to be short. Kat and Lindsay played checkers in the living room. Kat could not believe the level of skill with which the little girl played. Sam and Don talked about the best fishing spots and what hooks to use, while Connie and Pat watched the checker games and cheered on the competitors.

Sam put on his jacket and hat as he prepared to go back on duty. "Would you like to ride along, Kat?" he said, as an afterthought.

"You should go, Kat." Connie said. "I used to ride along, but now we have Lindsay. It'll give you a chance to see what Reno's all about. Unless you're too tired?"

"I think it would be interesting," Kat replied. "I slept most of the way over here, so I'm not tired at all."

She followed Sam out to the cruiser and hopped into the passenger seat. Sam drove around town, and gave out a couple of tickets for running red lights. "We can't have people running reds in town, Kat," he would say. "There are just too many pedestrians."

Kat found out that Sam had grown up in Las Vegas. He had met Connie at the University in Reno, and they had been here since. Connie and Lindsay were his pride and joy, and he talked constantly about them.

"There's a billy club under your seat, Kat. Just in case one of our passengers gets unruly. I usually wear it on my belt, but I can't drive with it. I'd rather not use my gun."

Sam got a call on his radio, so they sped off to the casino area. The casinos looked much older than the ones in Las Vegas, and there were far fewer of them.

They pulled over in front of a casino, where a cocktail waitress came to meet them. She led them to where a young man was passed out with his head on the table. Sam gently helped him to his feet and walked him to the car. He finally woke up enough to tell Sam where he lived, before getting into the back seat of the cruiser and falling asleep.

"College kid," Sam chuckled. "They get a little carried away sometimes." Sam drove the boy to his apartment and knocked on the door.

Another boy answered the door and helped his friend in, before thanking Sam for bringing him home. "He had an exam today," the boy said. "He'll pay the price tomorrow."

Sam drove back to the Strip and circled around a couple of times, when he got a call to notify him that three men had been shoplifting at a convenience store. Sam drove over and got a description of the men.

Kat was the first to spot three men ducking around a fence, and pointed them out to Sam, who drove slowly around the block.

"I know those punks," he said. "They must have just got out of jail." He pulled up beside them and got out of the car.

Kat watched as the three men crowded close to Sam, who did not seem to sense any danger. It was obvious to her that he could be in serious trouble if he did not act fast. She watched as he called for backup, as the men crowded closer around him.

Kat pulled the billy club from under her seat and quickly slipped from the car to the sidewalk. She stayed low in the shadows until she reached a trash barrel close to where the men stood. They were moving closer to Sam, beginning to slap and kick at him, while yelling obscenities at him.

Kat watched as she crouched in the shadow, like a mountain lion waiting to strike, the club held far behind her so it would obtain maximum speed and power by the time it hit its target. If things calmed down she would simply slip back into the car and wait for Sam as if nothing had happened.

One of the men clutched Sam and grabbed for his gun. Kat struck with lightning speed from her shadow. She hit the man below his outstretched arm, with her home run swing striking him in the ribs. As his arm dropped, she nailed him on the side of the head, dropping him like a sack of potatoes.

The other one swung at her, so she dropped and hit him on the side of the knee. As he dropped, she brought the club up under his chin, and then gave him one more on the ear as he fell to the ground.

The third man had his knife out and was charging at Kat. She brought the club down hard across his forearm, breaking the bones in its path as she sidestepped. Kat gave him an "Arnold Palmer" to the knees to take him down. Charley had given names to some of her moves, he had the "Arnold Palmer", the "Mickey Mantle", the Executioner", and many others.

Kat put the club into Sam's unsteady hand and got back into the car, just as the backup unit raced around the corner and screeched to a halt, uniformed men spilling out of it. The officers talked for a bit before they put the cuffs on the beaten men. When a wagon came, they loaded the men in, and Sam returned to the car.

"Thanks, Kat," he said, "I was beaten back there. If it hadn't have been for you, I wouldn't be here right now."

"Why didn't you pull your gun out, Sam?" asked Kat.

"I just can't, Kat. I knew I had to, but I still didn't," Sam replied.

"One of these times you may not be so lucky. Maybe you could transfer to another section."

"I'd just like to have my old job back," said Sam.

"What was that?" Kat asked.

"When I finished my degree in education, I taught school, while Connie finished University. When a job came open on the police force, I jumped at it, and we started a family."

"Why did you join the police force, Sam?" Kat asked.

"Well, Kat, both Connie's and my father were on the police force as we were growing up. We both thought it was the only way to support a family. To tell you the truth, I'm just not tough enough to deal with criminals. I hate it," Sam replied.

"That's a good fault to have," said Kat. "I saw how you handled that drunken boy back there. You have a lot of compassion, so maybe you need to return to teaching, rather than deal with the violence on the street."

"What do you think the folks would say, Kat?"

"They'd want the best for you, Connie and Lindsay. My Gramps used to tell me 'Stick with your knitting.' Maybe that's what you have to do, Sam."

Sam dropped Kat off at the house, and proceeded to the station to fill in the paperwork to cover the fact that Kat was even there. Those three were not about to say anything.

Don was the only one up when Sam stopped by the house in the morning. He went with Sam to return the cruiser to the station. Sam told Don what had happened during the night, and how Kat had saved him from injury and possible death. Nothing about Kat surprised Don any more. He had seen the little redhead in action and knew what she could do.

"Don," Sam finally said, "What would you say if I quit the force and went back to teaching Social Studies and History?"

Don thought for a few minutes, and finally said, "Sam, you're just too timid to be a cop. Pat and I worry about you. One of these nights, you aren't going to make it home. We'd be pulling for you all the way if you wanted to make a change."

Sam made his decision to leave the force on the spot. He had a standing offer from the local high school, and it was time to accept. They were both much happier when they returned to Sam's house.

Don picked the newspaper up off the doorstep on his way in, and took it into the living room. He stopped on the second page, reading an article over and over, before placing the newspaper beside Kat. Kat glanced down at the article and turned pale.

"Suspected Prostitution Ringleader Dead Of Drug Induced Heart Failure" read the headline. A picture of Nick was at the top of the page. The article stated how Nick had been found dead after a 911 call. A large amount of drugs and prostitution-related evidence was found at the scene. Kat breathed a sigh of relief when, at the end of the article, she read, "Foul play is not suspected."

Don watched Kat for signs of emotion during the entire time she read the article. He knew that she was somehow involved with Nick's death, but did not know how or why. He was quite certain that Kat was not a paid assassin, but she surely had the means. He saw that Kat was upset, and noted her relief when she learned she was not a suspect.

Don was glad that Nick was dead. He had been chasing him for years, but Nick was sly enough to always avoid prosecution, and had lots of money for his defence whenever the police got too close to convicting him. Don decided that Kat had done the world a favor, whatever her reasons. The world would be a safer place now for Connie and even little Lindsay.

Kat thought about the dream she had after Don had taken her home to his house. She had known all along that Nick was dead, but had refused to admit it to herself. Her life had changed after that night on the mountain.

She worried about her destiny. Had the bear really given her the mark of the warrior, as the elders had told her? Was she really on the other side?

She walked over to Don and gave him a hug. He looked at the sadness in her eyes, and hugged her back as if she were his own daughter. No words were spoken between them, but the meaning was very clear.

Connie came skipping down the stairs, looking happier than Kat had ever seen her. She made coffee, and Don and Kat joined her at the old round kitchen table.

"Thanks, Kat," she said. "Don told me how you helped him out last night. Lindsay and I depend on him a lot, and I can't imagine how life would be if he got hurt. Where did you learn to fight like that? Are you a black belt or something?"

Don listened intently, trying to determine if Kat was lying or not.

"No, Connie," she laughed. "My Gramps taught me, mostly out in the cow pasture. I used to think that everybody did that. I've been in a little town on the North Pacific Coast for the past couple of months, recovering from a bear attack. A young fellow and I practiced every day. We made a trade. He taught me how to fish and I taught him how to fight."

"You like to fish?" Don asked, hardly able to contain his excitement.

"Yes, I sure do," Kat replied. "I could sit and fish for hours. Funny, though, I find it calming just to sit and watch the water. It doesn't matter if I catch a fish or not."

"How about going today, Kat? They're biting at the lake not far from town."

"Sam will be sleeping today, so you can use his gear. You may as well go,

Kat. Dad loves to fish, but watch him, he can tell some pretty tall tales," Connie chuckled, winking at her dad.

Don and Kat loaded their fishing gear into the shiny old Chrysler, while Connie and Pat made them a lunch. Lindsay wanted to go with them, but had a soccer game. She waved at them as they went out of the driveway.

The landscape was different around Reno than it had been at Las Vegas. The hills were higher and the valley deeper. When they got to the lake, they carefully unpacked their fishing gear and waded into the cool water.

Don could tell a lot about a person by the way they fished. He prided himself in his ability to do so. He often told Pat that watching the way a person cast their line was like opening a window to their soul.

He watched carefully as Kat stripped some of the fly line off of the reel to float in the water beside her. Then she gently began to work the line back and forth in the air above her, never touching the smooth water.

Kat worked the line out further and further each time, until she finally let the fly touch down with the line settling softly onto the water behind it. As soon as the fly was on the water, Kat began to slowly retrieve it through the tiny circular ripples that it had left when it landed.

Don was certain there and then that Kat was not a criminal, but that she was actually quite a gentle person. He watched the power and determination with which she manoeuvred the long rod and line to land the tiny fly on the exact spot that she had chosen. He knew the feeling and began casting himself. They stood not far apart, the veteran police officer and the scarred little redhead, both contented and oblivious to the world around them.

"Must not be biting yet," Don said, as he waded back to shore. "Need some coffee to warm you up?"

"Sure," Kat replied, turning to wade out of the water and join him.

"You handle that fly pretty well, young lady," Don said with a smile.

"I had a good teacher," Kat replied. "After I'd been beat up by the bear, I stayed with a native family in Bella Coola, my friend Charley's family. He taught me how to fish."

"How do you get that fly to touch down so nice?" Don asked. "I've been trying to land it like that for years, but I still can't figure it out."

"I'll show you," Kat said as she picked up a rod and placed it carefully into Don's giant hand. "Don't bend your wrist, let your elbow and shoulder do all the movement," she said, as she held his hand and elbow in a firm grip, while simulating cast after cast.

Every time Don would lose his focus and let his wrist flex, she would scold him. Kat would only accept perfection, and eventually Don decided that if he was going to fish with her, that was the only way things were going to have to be. He was beginning to like her more and more.

Don's casts landed much better when he resumed fishing but Kat watched him like a hawk and scolded him each time he made a mistake. He laughed as he told her that he felt like he was back at boot camp.

Don finally hooked a big trout, and fought it carefully to where he was standing. Kat watched as he unhooked the fish and slid it back and forth in the water to revive it. The fish sped away the instant Don released it.

"Want to make a small wager?" Kat said, as she watched the trout speed away. "The person who catches the smallest fish buys supper for the whole family tonight."

"Are you sure you can afford it?" Don asked with a laugh.

"Yeah, but you realize that I've got a sign on my fly that says 'Big Fish Only'," Kat chuckled.

"Well, since we're in the gambling state, it would only be right, but you have to realize that you are competing against the lunker king." The bet was on as they measured fish after fish, teasing each other as they took turns winning.

"I'm getting hungry, and we'd better not take that lunch back home or we'll both be in trouble," Don said, as the sun rose high above them. They waded to shore and spread their lunch on a big rock between them. They ate quietly, and when they were finished they both lay back to enjoy the tranquillity.

"Tell me about your grandfather, Kat," Don finally said. "I don't mean to pry, but he sure sounds like an interesting man. I sure would have liked to meet him."

"Well," said Kat, "to me he was just my Gramps. He was an old cowboy with a heart of gold. He always wore a beat up old felt cowboy hat, not like the fancy black ones that you see around town but a stained old brown thing. He loved the ranch, and would spend hours watching the animals or looking at the mountains in the distance. He used to go into town with Gram in their old truck every few days, and visit with everybody they met. He and Gram were still best friends after all those years.

"Whenever anybody in the community needed help, they were right there to help them. Money was never of much importance to Gramps. He always told me that money and happiness weren't the same thing. You could have one without the other, unlike many people who think that it takes money to be happy.

"We'd go out into the pasture for my stick fighting lesson, and he'd tell me stories about amazing things. Since he died I've wondered if he was talking about things that he had actually done."

"Would you mind telling me one of those stories?" asked the old cop, as he lay there enjoying the heat from the sun.

"Sure," Kat replied, "but this stuff may be a bit confidential. You'll have to promise me that you'll never repeat it to anyone."

"I promise," Don replied, wondering what he was about to hear. "I'm a cop, remember? There are lots of things that I can't even tell Pat."

Kat began her story, "Gramps told me that one day some American soldiers in Vietnam got word that a Cambodian gang was trying to sell the bodies of some American soldiers killed in the war. The United States brings the bodies of their fallen soldiers home at all costs, so they arranged for two Secret Service men to go and investigate. The men were flown to Saigon on an undisclosed flight, and from there they made their way through Vietnam to the Cambodian border.

"When they got there, they quietly located the men who reportedly had the bodies, without revealing their identities. They negotiated a price and agreed to meet the following night to make the exchange. The Cambodians would bring the bodies back to Vietnam once the men had checked them and were satisfied.

"The following night, the men met, and the Americans were slipped back across the border and loaded into the back of a truck. They rode blindfolded for a long time, before the truck stopped and the blindfolds were taken off. A man took them over and showed them four mounds of earth, showing them a set of American dog tags, and it was then that he insisted on seeing the money. One of the Americans removed the money belt and showed them the money in United States bills as they had requested.

"It was then that things went wrong. The Cambodians pointed guns in their faces and laughed at them, calling them stupid Americans. They were taken down the hill to a small camp, where they were each put into a pit, which served as a jail cell. The pits were small, about 2 feet by 2 feet and only about 5 feet high so you couldn't stand or sit. They had bars made of sticks for a lid, that they kept tied down. The men were in constant agony, crouched in their cells, and were fed only a few grains of rice through the bars on rare occasions. The men were let out once every few days and marched around, as their captors watched their every move from behind the barrel of a submachine gun.

"One of the men discovered that he could catch rodents by putting a couple of grains of rice on his shoelace as a snare. He told this to the other man as they marched. The rats made for unappetising food but kept them from starvation. Their captors would laugh at them, and point at the graves on the hill above the camp.

"One day their guard spoke to them in English. He told them that they were being held for ransom and, if it didn't come soon, they would join the dead men on the hill. That was how they did it. He said Americans were stupid and had too much money anyway. The men worked on the sticks that covered their cells until one night a stick came loose. The man moved the others so nobody could tell that one was missing. He crouched quietly until he caught a big rat with his shoelace. He held the rat tightly by the lid of his cell and squeezed it so it would squeal. When the guard came over and looked down into the cell the man brought the sharp end of the stick up into his throat and killed him by strangling him, reaching up through the bars as the man lay there.

"He pried the lid open with the stick and threw the dead guard into the pit, then ran over and let the other American out. He crawled up the guard tower and silenced the guard with his stick and shoelace, never making a sound that would alert the camp. Then they crawled up past the graves into the jungle. They stopped at the graves to swear an oath. They promised the dead soldiers that they would be back to bring them home.

"The men hid by day and traveled at night, until one night they slipped back across the Cambodian border. They were eventually picked up by a group of U.S. soldiers, who took them to their base. They couldn't tell anybody who they were and what they were doing there, so they made up a story about being left behind when their helicopter came under fire when they were setting up a heavy gun up front. They said they'd hid in the trees, and when things calmed down after the chopper was gone, they walked out. They ate a huge meal and settled into their bunks. When everyone was asleep they slipped away in the dark, not wanting to blow their cover, knowing that by the next day their story would be checked out.

"The men worked their way, undiscovered, all the way to Saigon where they met their contact. They were whisked back to the States, where they met with the President himself for debriefing. One of the men couldn't handle the pressure of being held in the pit and the starvation, so he took his own life shortly after. The other man regained his strength quickly. He had made a map on a piece of bark so he could find his way back into the camp. He was authorized to take a team of Green Berets with him to recover the bodies.

"They trained from morning until night, with silence being of utmost priority. They trained with clubs and knives, as they knew that a single shot would alert their enemies for miles. When it was time, the small group quietly boarded the plane on American soil, and jumped out high over Cambodia, each with a knife clenched in his teeth. They landed silently on the hill above the graves, then crept down to the camp. The Secret Service man slipped in and silenced the man in the guard tower, while the Green Berets attacked the men in the barracks with clubs, knives and strangle cords.

"Within the hour, every one of the enemy lay there lifeless. They checked the pits, only to find two new soldiers occupying them. The small attack team made their way back up the hill to where the graves were located, and carefully dug the bodies up. The parachutes had been specially sewn for this mission, with straps and handles for carrying the bodies, which were placed in them.

"The men made their way back to the border without any casualties, having to make several silent attacks on the enemy with their clubs to ensure their secrecy. They crossed back across the border to Vietnam on their bellies, dragging their makeshift body bags behind them in the darkness. They had a rescue plan this time, so helicopters picked them up and flew them to an aircraft carrier that was laying way out past the Mekong Delta.

"After that, I'm not sure what happened to them all. Gramps told me that one a lot. He said that a stick may save your life one day, just like it did for the guy in the story." Kat lay back and stared at the blue sky.

"That's quite the yarn, Kat. I'd just bet it's true. The Secret Service man must have been your grandfather. That would explain a lot," Don said.

"Yeah," Kat replied, "but we'd better get at it so you can catch that minnow."

They waded back into the lake and began trying to lure the hungry fish into biting again, when Kat asked Don, "What would you do if you were me?"

"I'm not sure that I understand your question, Kat," Don said politely.

Kat said, "Well, Don, I've just finished high school, and I've got my whole life ahead of me. I like being a waitress, but I don't think that's what I want to do my whole life. You've seen more than I have, so I was wondering if you'd have any suggestions. I really don't know what I want."

Don thought for a few minutes as he cast his line, before he finally answered her.

"Well, Kat," he said, "Connie asked me the very same question a few years ago, but her life was a lot different from yours. You are very mature for your age. Sometimes, when I look at you, I think that you are carrying the weight of the world on your shoulders. You seem to think of everyone but yourself.

"I know for sure that you should stay away from the rougher parts of town. You're a good fighter, but, if you keep it up, one of these days you're going to catch a stray bullet. I know you were somehow involved with Nick's death, but I don't want you to tell me anything. I can't repeat what I've never been told. Even under oath, nobody can make me surmise anything. You need to go to a place where life is simple, maybe even the ranch where you grew up. That way trouble won't be so likely to find you.

"You need to get an education, Kat. It's hard for girls these days to get a decent job without an education. The choices become yours, like how you earn your living, where you decide to live, and such. Don't take something that's going to land you behind a desk for the rest of your life, because you need to be in the outdoors. Whatever you do, Kat, make sure that the decision is your own."

"Thanks, Don," Kat said, as she settled her fly onto the smooth water. "I guess I knew that all along, but I just needed some reassurance. When I get back, I'm going to go to the University and pick out something I like. Maybe I can find something that will help me start a business in Bella Coola. Charley and I talked about starting a lodge and taking people fishing on the river. We could hire the local people to help us. We'd need guides and cooks and stuff. We could take hiking tours up the petroglyphs and show them things in the rain forest that they would never see otherwise."

"It sounds like you've already got a plan in the works, Kat, and it sounds like a mighty good one to me. Pat and I could move up and help you run it. Shucks, you wouldn't even have to pay me. I've just got a couple of years until I retire, and plan on just fishing anyway. It would be perfect."

"You'd love it there, Don," Kat said. "You could walk down to the river and catch supper every day."

Just then the tip of Kat's rod began to quiver, so she pulled it in, thinking that a frog or something had caught on her fly. As she pulled it in, she saw what must be the smallest fish in the entire lake, hooked onto the fly. It looked like it would be more at home in a goldfish bowl.

"Do you want to take it home and have it mounted?" Don laughed hysterically.

"Wouldn't take up too much space on the wall."

They laughed as they released the tiny fish back into the lake, and were still chuckling as they packed their gear, both knowing that Kat's catch could not be outdone.

"I'm the champion small fish catcher, so I'm buying supper," Kat laughed as they headed home. Kat realized that she and Don had become very good friends in the short time they had known each other. They had had a good day at the lake, and had enjoyed each other's company. They schemed and planned about the fishing lodge all the way home, like a couple of children setting out on a great adventure.

Kat cleaned up the fishing gear and stowed it all away before she went to clean up for supper. Don and Sam were having an evening cocktail, while the girls crowded around an intense game of checkers.

Connie was glad that they were going out for supper. Her life was a bit hectic right now, but she could not be happier. Don would be able to leave late tonight, and would only have to work a short late shift in Las Vegas. Sam had a friend who ran an Italian restaurant, so that was their evening destination.

When Kat came out a long while later, all heads turned and stared. Kat did not look anything like she had that afternoon, dressed in sneakers and a track suit, with her hair askew. She now wore a long evening gown that Nika had sent with her and not a hair was out of place.

"You look like a million bucks," said Don. "What ever happened to the little redhead that was my fishing partner today?"

Lindsay ran over and held her hand as she smiled up at her. "You could win the Miss Universe contest looking like that," Pat said, as they headed down the road in the old Chrysler.

Kat was not familiar with dining anywhere but at home, but Nika and Brenda had coached her well. She handled herself with grace and elegance, which impressed her new friends. Kat was not entirely sure what she was eating at times, but it tasted very good. Lindsay insisted on sitting next to her, so she could tell her about the soccer game she had played earlier that day.

When supper was over, Don stood and made a toast to their new friend Kat. He told everyone how he had nearly misjudged the young girl when he had first seen her walking down the sidewalk in Las Vegas with a limp, using a broken hockey stick as a cane. He apologized for the error in judgement and thanked Kat for going fishing with him. They all touched glasses and drank the toast.

"I've got an announcement to make too," said Sam, as he stood up and pushed his chair back. "I gave my notice today. I will be ending my short career as a police officer. I've been accepted as a Social Studies teacher at the high school, and I'll start in a couple of weeks. The teacher there just up and quit, so they needed someone right away, so I said yes."

Everyone clapped and drank a toast to Sam's new endeavor. Lindsay was not sure what they were all talking about.

"Now we have another announcement," Sam said, as Connie stood beside him. The others stared at them as Connie cleared her throat, too embarrassed to speak. She finally gathered up the courage to say, "We're going to have a baby."

Lindsay obviously knew what that meant, as she ran around to hug her mother and begin her questioning, while the others drank another toast.

"If it's a girl we're going to name her Kathy," Connie said, beaming at Kat.

This had been a very happy evening for all of them. They all knew that Sam was not cut out for being a police officer, and were excited about the baby. Lindsay had not stopped interrogating her mother since she had made her announcement. She was so happy she could not sit still for a second.

Kat, the only one up, had the coffee on when Pat came down and sat at the table beside her.

"I have to thank you, Kat," she said.

"You don't have to thank me," Kat replied. "I should be thanking you for making me so welcome. I sure wouldn't have been this happy if I'd hung out on the Strip for a week."

"No, Kat," Pat said. "I have to thank you for possibly saving Sam's life, and for what you've done for Don. He's a new man since he's been around you. His family is raised and he's getting ready to retire soon. I think he figures that nobody needs him any more.

"That was, until he met you. All he could talk about last night was going to Canada and helping you build your fishing lodge. He sat up and planned all night. This morning, he told me we're buying a motor home and heading for Bella Coola. Maybe buy a house and settle down there. I've been trying to get him to travel, but he'll hardly leave the place since Connie left, just over here to visit for a while."

"Thanks, Pat," Kat said. "What do you think about our scheme?"

"I like it," replied Pat. "We need something to do when we retire, and we both love the wilderness. With Sam back teaching, they can spend the summers with us, then we can come here to visit in the winter. It would be perfect."

They visited in the kitchen until the others finally got up.

"Would you like to go to Lake Tahoe today, Kat?" Don asked, as he poured himself a cup of coffee.

"Sure, I'd love to," she replied.

Don would have rather gone back to the lake, but he promised Pat and Lindsay that he would take them for a drive. They drove first to Virginia City, where they toured all of the old buildings.

Virginia City had once been the hub of a gold and silver mining area. Kat could picture the prospectors coming in from their claims, leading their burros. Fortunes had been won and lost at the Faro tables in the old gambling houses.

They all bellied up to a shiny old bar for a Coke and ice cream, and Lindsay was allowed to order for everyone. The bartender teased her as he brought their drinks. She sat as tall as she could on her bar stool, proudly organizing Kat and her grandparents.

A photographer convinced them to have their group picture taken. They dressed up in old fashioned clothing, and posed with Lindsay sitting on Kat's knee and Don and Pat holding a pitchfork between them. When they saw their picture, they all laughed at themselves. They looked like they were right out of the Old West. Pat led them into every shop in the old town to look at the artifacts and antiques.

They went to Carson City next, for a look around, before they proceeded to Lake Tahoe. Kat loved the mountains, and noticed the changes in her surroundings as they climbed. The changes she had seen between the desert at Las Vegas and the mountains of Lake Tahoe were incredible. The forests reminded her of the evergreen foothills just west of the ranch.

Snow was beginning to cover the hills, and was piled high beside the highway. Lake Tahoe looked like a scene from a Hollywood movie. Pat led them back and forth through every shop in town, but Kat could sense that Don was not much of a shopper.

They stopped for lunch before Don pointed the old Chrysler back to Reno. Kat and Lindsay fell asleep in the back.

"Would you like to come along with me tonight, Kat?" Sam asked. "I only have to work until midnight, and I only have a few shifts left."

"Sure, I'd love to," Kat said. "I have to fly home tomorrow night, and I'd like to see everything," and went out to the cruiser with Sam. They toured around town, giving out traffic tickets and the odd reprimand for jaywalking. Sam was driving around the residential areas looking for prowlers when he got a call to go to the station for a meeting.

"Must be setting up a sting or something. I'll have to drop you off at home, Kat," he said.

"How about just dropping me off by the casinos? I'll take a cab home."

"Better yet," Sam said, "I'm off at midnight so I can pick you up."

"Sure," said Kat. "Comstock, just past midnight."

Sam dropped her off and Kat watched as he drove out of sight.

She wandered in and out of the casinos, stopping long enough to watch a hand of cards or wait until the ball of the spinning roulette wheel rolled into the winning slot. The bells rang and lights flashed, as people fed money into the one armed bandits.

She watched as a young woman won a jackpot and the coins poured into the tray. The woman's friends gathered around her, excitedly bringing containers for her winnings. Kat moved on when the excitement was over.

When she got to the furthest casino, she walked back across the tracks and took a street just off the Strip back towards the action.

Kat had walked a few blocks when she saw a lineup of people in front of an older building. As she got closer, she saw that the line was composed mostly of rough looking men, but in their midst was a middle aged woman holding the hand of a young girl. The sign above the door said "Catholic Mission."

Being the curious person that she was, Kat stood across from the mission in the shadows, wondering what she was seeing. A tall man stepped out of the side door and walked along the lineup, talking to people as he went along. He eventually walked across the dimly lit street to where Kat stood, and stared quietly at the old mission. "May I help you?" he finally asked Kat, as he turned to face her.

Kat looked at him carefully, noticing that he looked like neither a local businessman nor a tourist. "I was just wondering what this place is and who those people are," Kat replied. "I'm just looking around town and happened to be going by."

"I will be more than happy to tell you about this place, young lady," the man said. "This is a Mission which is run by the Catholic Church. We feed the homeless here, and provide them with a warm, safe place to spend the night. Most of the people who come here have no money and no home. We do what we can do to help them, but our home is a humble one, and our resources are limited. My name is Father Ronaldo Spurrelli, and this is how I serve the Lord."

He opened his arms wide toward the mission as he bowed deeply.

"Is that woman with the little girl homeless?" asked Kat.

"Yes, dear," Father Spurrelli said. "She comes with one of the most saddening stories of anyone who has passed through our care. I met her the day we buried her husband. Would you like me to tell you how she came here?"

"Yes, I'd like to hear it," said Kat.

"She told me that she had met her husband in California, at the place where she worked. He was much older than she was, but they fell in love and were married. The next year, they had the little girl that you see there. They had a nice home, where she stayed to raise the child while he made the living.

"Last year, they flew to Florida for their vacation, and her husband was offered a very good job. They sold all of their possessions, and left California last month to move to Florida. Their only mistake was that they stopped overnight here in Reno. They booked into a motel and her husband went to the casino for a while. That was the last time she saw him.

"Apparently, he had been an addicted gambler earlier in his life, but she knew nothing about it. He lost all of the money from the sale of their house and other possessions. Then he pawned everything they brought with them, and lost that too. The next day, he took his own life. When the police informed her, she was completely devastated. Her life had completely fallen apart. She had no money or home, and he had even sold their pickup. The city buried him in a pauper's grave and I helped with the funeral service. That's where I first met them."

"That's quite a story," said Kat. "It must be terribly hard for her and her little girl." The doors opened and the people began to slowly file in. "Are they just now being allowed in?" asked Kat.

"Yes," he said, "we can't allow anyone to live here, so we open the doors in the evening and clear everybody out again in the morning. Would you like to come in and see for yourself what we do here?"

"Sure," Kat said. She followed closely as he walked up the stairs to where the woman was handing out sandwiches and drinks.

"Hi, I'm Rhonda," the woman said, offering a sandwich and coffee to Kat.

"I'm Kat," she said, accepting the coffee, but refusing the sandwich.

"I don't know what I'd do without Rhonda," Father Spurrelli said. "She spends her every spare moment helping the homeless."

He led Kat to a table in the corner, where she sat down across from the lady with the young girl. Then he went to help Rhonda.

Kat quietly sipped her coffee until the woman spoke. "Hi, my name is Eileen, and this is my daughter, Becky."

"My name's Kathy but people call me Kat."

"What brings you to this place?" Eileen asked.

"Oh, I just met Father Spurrelli and he invited me in. He told me about your unfortunate circumstances, Eileen. It sure must be hard for you."

"Mom, can I go help Rhonda?" Becky asked.

"As long as you stay out of her way," she said, watching Becky race over to where Rhonda was serving lunch. Rhonda handed her a full pot of coffee to pass around to this evening's clients.

"Yes, it's hard. I've never been wealthy before, but I've never been this broke either," Eileen said. "I'm a registered nurse, but I haven't worked in a few years. I've got a job to go to, at the hospital up in Billings, Montana, if I can get there, but I don't even have enough for a bus ticket for Becky and myself.

"My folks live on a ranch out past Roundup, not far from Billings, but they don't even have a phone. They're just getting by on the ranch, so they can't afford to help us. Enough complaining, though, Kat. We're lucky to be alive, and to have met Father Spurrelli and Rhonda. How about you Kat, how's your life going?" She could not help but notice the deep scars on Kat's face and knew that her life could not have been entirely easy.

Becky came by and refilled Kat's cup with fresh, hot coffee and a big smile.

"I came to Las Vegas for a vacation, and wound up meeting the nicest people you could imagine. They brought me over here with them for a few days, so I'm just snooping around. I'm not much for the gambling, and just happened to be passing by when Father Spurrelli walked out and invited me in."

A young man strummed his guitar and started singing a country song. All heads turned, and a few of the men began to sing along. Kat touched the envelope in her pocket of her jeans, containing the money from the punks. She pulled it out and slid it across the table, concealed under her hands, to Eileen.

Eileen took the envelope and quietly peeked inside it, before tucking it under the table. "I can't accept this," she told Kat.

"No, it's yours. I've been looking for a home for this money, and now I've found it. Take Becky to Billings and get yourself set up there. You can get your job and get Becky back in school. Becky pours a mean cup of coffee, and I might need one if I ever pass through Billings."

Eileen held the envelope below the table, and discreetly thumbed through the money. "But there's over four thousand dollars here!" she exclaimed.

"That's good," Kat replied. "I have to go now. Nice meeting you."

Father Spurrelli was busy calming down an elderly gentleman when Kat left, so she just waved and smiled, and he gave her a wink that nobody noticed.

Eileen waved Father Spurrelli over when he was finished and showed him the money. "Should I keep it?" she asked.

"By all means," Father Spurrelli said. "It was given to you unconditionally. Use it wisely, to help give yourself and your daughter the life that you deserve."

Becky came over and jumped up on the chair that Kat had been sitting on. "Where did the angel go, Mom?" she asked.

"What angel?" her mother asked.

"The one that was sitting here, right in this chair," she said. "Can't you tell an angel when you see one, Mom?"

"No, this was my first one."

"What do you think, Father Spurrelli?" Becky asked.

"The Lord works in mysterious ways," he said, "Very mysterious ways."

Sam pulled up to the sidewalk where Kat stood, and Kat hopped in.
"How was your evening, Kat?" he said, as he drove.

"It was interesting," she replied. "I went through all of the casinos, and watched the people gambling for a while. Some of them sure get into it. Then I came back down the side street, and wound up at a Catholic Mission."

"So you met Father Spurrelli," Sam laughed.

"I sure did," Kat replied. "He took me into the Mission, so I could see what it was all about. What would those people do without him and Rhonda?"

"I really don't know, Kat, we'd be lost without him. I pick up people all the time who've fallen through the cracks, and take them over to the Mission. He takes them in and helps them. Quite a piece of work, that old boy."

"I really couldn't help wondering how people could be gambling fortunes away, while a block away there are folks without enough to eat," said Kat.

"You'll never answer that question, Kat," Sam said. "I see it every day and it never changes. There's a line-up at the mission every night." Sam pulled into the driveway and they walked quietly into the house.

It was like a line of army ants packing things to the old Chrysler. Kat was amazed at how much would fit into the trunk. Pat was eventually satisfied that all was aboard, so the packing operation ground to a halt. Kat sat in the back seat as they drove away, waving back to the happy little family standing in the driveway.

Don and Pat sang along to Simon and Garfunkel as they drove down the highway. "Hard to believe I'll soon be retired," said Don. "Seems that song came out yesterday."

"The world sure has changed a lot since we were kids, Kat. The Vietnam war was always on our minds when we were young," Pat said. "Now we have different worries."

THE MUSHROOM PICKER

Don swung the Chrysler into an R.V. lot and they all got out. A salesman sauntered over with a huge smile and an outstretched arm that almost shook poor Don to pieces.

"We're going to Canada next summer and need something reliable," Don said.

"Yeah, I've got just the one for you," the salesman assured him. "It's pretty rough country up there. Not much for roads or anything, and it's a long way between towns. People tell me they're a bunch of hillbillies. You ever been up there?"

"No," said Don, winking and grinning at Kat. "This will be our first trip."

"You'll need a unit that's big enough to bring everything you need with you. Folks tell me those Canadians up there don't even eat very good. Live on moose and such. Not much grows up there, 'cause it snows all the time. Yeah, you better get one of these here diesels." He led them through some beautiful machines, until Don excused himself and told him they would think about it.

Don laughed until he could hardly breathe when they were back in the car. "I think that fellow needs to get out more," he said. "He'd say anything to make a sale."

"I knew I was missing something," Kat laughed. "Anybody around here sell a good mooseburger?"

"What is it really like up there, Kat?" Don asked. "I probably shouldn't be laughing at the salesman. I've never even been north of here."

Kat spent the next hour, as they drove, carefully describing the country she loved, in detail. When she finally finished, she felt a twinge of homesickness, and was glad she was going home tonight.

Don checked out every R.V. lot between Reno and Las Vegas. By the time they reached the house, he was becoming somewhat of an expert.

"I've never seen him so committed to anything," Pat said privately to Kat. "He's determined that we're going to Canada this summer. Thanks again, Kat. I've not seen him so happy since we were teenagers."

Kat gathered her things, loaded them into her luggage, and got ready to leave for the airport.

Just before they left, Don called Kat into his den. He pointed to a broken and battered hockey stick, mounted on the wall among the trophies and medals that he had acquired through the years.

"I'll never forget that little redheaded girl that I first saw limping down the sidewalk. I'll never again be too quick to judge anyone, and I still can't believe what I watched you do with that broken stick. I'll always keep it as a reminder. If I ever feel sorry for myself, all I'll have to do is look at it, and I'll see the brighter side and my fears will go away."

Kat watched as a tear ran down his cheek, and now understood what Pat had been talking about. Don was growing older, and close to retirement. His family did not need him as much any more. Kat knew now that this rugged old officer of the law had been afraid of the unknown, but he had never shown fear in his life. Hopefully he was better now.

Kat waved back at Don and Pat, once she had passed through security. She bought a travel magazine to read as she waited for her boarding call. When it was finally announced, she made her way to her window seat. The plane was backed carefully out until they could taxi out to the runway. Noise from the turbines filled the cabin as the pilot pushed the throttles and held the brakes. When he was satisfied, he released the brakes and the jet raced down the runway. The nose came up and the plane began to climb, until the pilot banked and Kat could see the lights from the City of Sins beneath her.

Her heartbeat quickened as she thought about coming home. Dad and Nika would be at the airport to meet her. The weather channel said a Chinook was blowing in to warm things up a bit, so the cold would not be such a shock when she got off the plane.

Nika would insist on driving her old Brockle, and would probably jerk the clutch whenever she tried to take off. Dad would sit quietly and just smile over at Kat.

The questions would be steady, so Kat would have to be very careful not to slip and tell them everything. That had to be saved for the right moment, when they were sitting on the top rail. That's where the most important conversations in the Townsend family took place, she thought, grinning to herself.

Kat opened her travel magazine and began to read about Hawaii. She was very tired from the long drive, so her eyelids began to flutter.

Soon Kat was on a tropical beach, watching the waves gently lapping on the shore. Trade winds caused the giant palm trees to sway back and forth.

THE MUSHROOM PICKER

Somewhere in the distance, she heard children laughing, as they did the Huki Lau to a Hawaiian guitar. A sailboat slowly drifted along the horizon beside the brightly setting sun.

~ The End ~

Printed in the United States
35419LVS00002B/436-453